P9-CFU-566

A
BEAUTIFUL
EVIL

Also by Kelly Keaton

Darkness Becomes Her

A Beautiful Evil

KELLY KEATON

Simon Pulse
New York London Toronto Sydney New Delhi

This book is a work of fiction. Any references to historical events, real people, or real locales are used fictitiously. Other names, characters, places, and incidents are the product of the author's imagination, and any resemblance to actual events or locales or persons, living or dead, is entirely coincidental.

SIMON PULSE
An imprint of Simon & Schuster Children's Publishing Division
1230 Avenue of the Americas, New York, NY 10020
First Simon Pulse hardcover edition February 2012

For information about special discounts for bulk purchases, please contact Simon & Schuster Special Sales at 1-866-506-1949 or business@simonandschuster.com.
The Simon & Schuster Speakers Bureau can bring authors to your live event. For more information or to book an event contact the Simon & Schuster Speakers Bureau at 1-866-248-3049 or visit our website at www.simonspeakers.com.
The text of this book was set in Adobe Caslon.
Manufactured in the United States of America
2 4 6 8 10 9 7 5 3
Library of Congress Cataloging-in-Publication Data
Keaton, Kelly.
A beautiful evil / by Kelly Keaton. — 1st Simon Pulse hardcover ed.
p. cm.
Sequel to: Darkness becomes her.
Summary: In the post-apocalyptic city of New 2, Ari Selkirk, who has discovered that she is a descendant of Medusa, is trying to keep at bay the evil growing inside her, but the goddess Athena will stop at nothing to possess Ari's power, provoking a monumental battle between good and evil.
ISBN 978-1-4424-0927-9 (hardcover)
[1. Good and evil—Fiction. 2. Supernatural—Fiction. 3. Monsters—Fiction. 4. Athena (Greek deity)—Fiction. 5. New Orleans (La.)—Fiction.] I. Title.
PZ7.K22525Be 2012
2011016580
ISBN 978-1-4424-0929-3 (eBook)

For Cheryl Hogan,
an amazingly strong, loving, wonderful human being.
Thanks for supporting me in all my wild endeavors
(and for showing me the mushrooms that fairies
stand under when it rains, the Lady Slippers
they sleep in, and the stumps of old trees
they call castles). Love you, Mom!

A
BEAUTIFUL
EVIL

One

"Everyone knows what you are now. Question is, Selkirk, will you live up to their expectations or be the complete failure I think you really are?"

My pulse thundered like a herd of galloping horses. Sweat rolled down my back, dampening my shirt and the waistline of my jeans. Tiny wisps of hair stuck to my face and neck. I kept my eyes shut and dug my short fingernails into the wrist I held tightly, wishing I could inflict some pain . . . or better yet, make him shut the—

"Do it!" he snarled, his breath fanning across my forehead.

A head butt might work. Bone would crack. Blood would flow. Sweet satisfaction—and even sweeter silence—would ensue. "I'm *trying*," I said through gritted teeth.

I squeezed my eyes closed tighter than they already were. For forty-five minutes I'd been "trying," and that was about forty-four minutes too long to stay in a room with Bran Ramsey.

C'mon, Ari. Concentrate!

If I could figure out how to control my power and use it at will, even just a tiny bit, my training session would be done for the day and I could rejoin the nontortured students at Presby.

Bran's calloused hand clamped around my throat. My eyes flew open. What the hell? He squeezed hard, his fingers encircling my neck almost completely. I struggled, questioning him with my look, unable to do anything more than make small wheezing noises.

"You're not trying," he growled deeply, stepping on my toes. "You're too scared to try. You even *smell* scared. You make me sick, Selkirk."

He wasn't letting go.

Pressure built behind my eyes and in my face. My lungs strained. I pulled at his hand. I slapped. I kicked. I punched at his arms and chest, unable to reach his head. But it didn't matter. None of it mattered. Going up against Bran was like trying to beat up an oak tree.

My chest burned. Couldn't . . . breathe . . .

Bran leaned close, his nose almost touching mine, the brown in his eyes going darker and meaner. "What are you going to do now, god-killer?"

White fuzz began to ring my vision. My arms went limp. He released me with a shove. I stumbled back in disbelief, gasping for air. I braced my hands on my knees, concentrating on each painful breath—in and out, in and out—until the dizziness ebbed and I was able to straighten.

An open-handed smack landed on the back of my head. I ducked, my arms going protectively over my head. "Stop it! Jesus! Are you insane?!"

"Fight me."

He moved too quickly for me to defend myself. A boot to the back of my knee sent me crumbling to the floor. My hands slapped hard against the mat. This was really starting to get old. "Stop it, Bran. I'm done, okay?"

I'd been trained as a bail bondsman by my last foster parents, Bruce and Casey, but nothing had prepared me for this. This was . . . different. This was removed, cold, and impatient. This didn't inspire confidence, and so far it hadn't taught me a damn thing at all. This was simply an exercise to show me what it felt like to be a mouse to Bran's maniacal cat.

I was almost too afraid to get up, knowing he wasn't finished with me. I lifted my head, swiped the sweat from my brow with my arm, and glanced at the clock. Five more minutes until the bell rang.

Five more minutes. I chanted those three words over and over as I straightened and faced him.

Bran stood in the center of the room, feet braced apart, thick arms folded over his chest, one dark eyebrow cocked up. There was no sheen of sweat on his tanned face. No dampness to his wavy sable brown hair.

"I thought you were supposed to *teach* me, not try to kill me," I forced out through my sore throat.

"Semantics." He flicked a glance at the clock and smirked, telling me with a look exactly how much damage he could do in the next four minutes.

"I'm done, okay?" I said tiredly. "Can we just . . . stop?"

"Stop what?"

I rolled my eyes, letting my frustrations flow into my words. "Uh, gee, I don't know. Stop baiting me, stop pushing me, stop hitting me, stop being a supreme *asshole.*" There, I said it. And it felt good. Damn good. It wasn't like he was going to take it easy on me anyway.

A lethal grin pulled his lips apart. "Make me."

The gleam in his dark eyes—it was like he was dying for someone to finally give him some decent action. And that someone, he had decided, was me. It didn't matter that I was a student and he was a demigod/security specialist/one of the nine Novem heads. Semantics, right?

I stepped forward, knowing I could probably draw this out until the bell rang. I was, if nothing else, experienced in the art of toughing it out. There were ways a body could turn and move so that the blows wouldn't hurt so much. I took up a defensive position.

Bran's hand shot out. "No. Make me . . . with your mind."

His words sank in and I snorted, arching one eyebrow to match his cocky expression. "I don't exactly see you using yours."

He moved in a blur, so fast I didn't have time to tense before he had me spun around and shoved front-first against the far wall, one arm twisted behind my back and the side of my face squished into the oak paneling.

Shock stole my breath, but only for a second before the anger rushed in, forcing away my surprise and pushing my blood pressure higher. The clock was ticking. *Tough it out.*

Then he breathed purposefully on my neck and chuckled, dropping his voice to a husky tone. "I suppose we could try another sort of tactic. . . ."

He was too close. Too pressed up against me. Too in my space. I was trapped. Completely trapped. Oh God. A sick wave rolled over my stomach.

I felt it then, uncoiling, waking, and my fear turned to panic. I mumbled words like a prayer: *"No, no, no."*

Bran laughed softly. "Yes."

My curse stirred, rising like smoke from my toes to my scalp, swirling, twisting, pushing painfully into places never meant to be filled. Every nerve shivered, every fine hair stood up, every ounce of flesh crawled as though a swarm of bugs scattered along my skin.

My body went stiff, bracing against the inevitable rise of power until I couldn't bear the sensations anymore. *Goddamn you, Bran!*

It rushed the rest of the way in. Energetic. Alive. Aware. My curse, the gorgon, was a living shadow inside me.

I screamed and twisted from Bran's hold, vaguely acknowledging that he let me, and grabbed his neck. His eyes were hard, daring. Our gazes locked as a tingling sensation shot down my arm and into my hand. It was cold, heartless, vicious. . . . Movement, like the softest breeze, began beneath my scalp. Slither—*No, no, no.*

I screamed again, against the horror, finally finding enough strength to shove Bran back.

Then it was over.

My curse retreated, leaving me slumped against the wall, my eyes wide and glassy, heart beating so fast I thought it might burst.

Bran stood very still. His neck and the skin over his jawbone were white—unnaturally white—marble. Me. I'd done that. His dark eyes bored into mine, intense, but somehow calm and confident. His skin color slowly returned, and his shoulders relaxed.

"And *that*, Ari Selkirk," he said smugly, rubbing his jaw, "is called trying."

He strolled to the far corner to take a swig of water from his bottle. Still stunned by what I'd done, I watched his throat work as he drank deeply. I knew what I could do, had felt the same sensations before, but it was still a shock to the system; it wasn't something I'd ever get used to. And I didn't want to.

Bran set the bottle down, swiped a hand over his mouth, then leaned casually against the table in the corner to study me. "Now that we know your power stirs from fear and adrenaline, we have something to work with. Don't make me push you that far again. It's . . . distasteful. Soon you'll be able to control it without giving in to those unnecessary emotions. But"—he shrugged—"I suppose it's a decent enough start for your first day of training."

The bell rang.

And I just stood there staring at him, amazed by how he could sound so blasé after all that.

"We'll work again tomorrow." He nodded to the door. "Now get lost."

I headed for my backpack on the floor by the door, my legs so weak I was surprised they even worked. My hand trembled as I grabbed the strap to my bag, slung it over my shoulder, and left the room the other students at Presby had dubbed The Dungeon.

Two

I LEFT BRAN'S WITH ONE GOAL IN MIND: TO GET OUT OF PRESBY. I had one more class left, but it didn't matter because I was done with the school and its crazy curriculum of normal and paranormal studies. At least for today.

My steps were quick, but not so quick as to attract attention. My head stayed down and I moved with a kind of reserved desperation. Bran's way of bringing out my power had stripped all my defenses, leaving me shaken, exposed, and on the edge of reliving old hurts I'd rather forget. I felt wooden as I navigated the maze of students, then down the hall and through the tall double doors of the Presbytère.

Emerging from Presby's shadowed arched gallery and into

the sun was like stepping into a different world with an entirely different vibe.

The wide pedestrian street that ran in front of the school, St. Louis Cathedral, and the Cabildo was filled with outdoor vendors—florists, artists, fortune-tellers, and retailers with gobs of Mardi Gras beads and masks.

I crossed the pavement as a three-man jazz band began belting out a loud, energetic tune. The sun's heat emanated from the bricks and stone, and a decent late-winter breeze blew in from the Mississippi, which was only a few hundred feet beyond Jackson Square. I couldn't see the river, but the scent of the muddy water and Gulf coast was unmistakable.

I'd gone from the stuffy halls of Presby and into the beating heart of the French Quarter.

The grounds inside the square were the peaceful, contented part of the Quarter's heart—an oasis of green grass and trees and secluded benches surrounded by the spikes of black iron fencing, and in the center the restored statue of a mounted Andrew Jackson.

I found a long bench in a quiet corner. The bushes behind me were contained by the fence separating the square from the street. A tree provided shade, and I was far enough off the brick path that no one would see my angry, frustrated tears.

They'd just see a sweat-soaked girl in dark clothes with

strange white hair lying on the bench, arm covering her face.

Just a girl. Resting on a bench.

I'd had to wait three days before I could even start classes, and I'd spent most of that time pacing, biting my nails, getting very little sleep, and thinking of Violet and my father. I'd *wanted* this so badly I'd crashed the Novem's Council of Nine meeting and demanded to attend Presby.

The thought made me laugh. I wanted to learn everything I could about Athena—how to find her, defeat her, and save those I loved. I wanted to be as prepared as possible. Yet there was that frustrated, highly impatient part of me that just wanted to say "screw it" and go in with guns blazing.

Only I didn't know where to go.

My worries over Violet, my father, and my curse—which I'd yet to come to terms with—were eating away at me, and I was letting them; I was losing sight of my purpose, losing my focus.

My focus had to stay on Presby, on knowledge, training, and the secret library.

The Novem's school was all inclusive—K–12 and a four-year private college, which took up not only the Presbytère building but also several of the buildings along both sides of St. Ann Street. All the Novem's knowledge, all its resources, were right here. . . .

And I hated to admit it, but one of the biggest resources was Bran the Bastard.

I was pissed at him, pissed that he'd pushed me to my breaking point, to the very heart of what I feared most. But in the end, he'd been right to do it. He knew what he was doing, and even with only one training session under my belt, he was by far the best I'd ever trained with. I knew my anger was misplaced, knew it was really fear.

The one sliver of hope I had of defeating Athena was my curse, and yet . . . the idea of tapping into that *thing* inside me was horrifying.

I didn't want it, and deep down I was terrified it would take over, that if I started messing with my power now, I'd become a monster before the curse fully manifested at twenty-one. That once I let the gorgon out, I'd never be able to control it.

I wanted to stay . . . me.

A sob caught in my throat as a wave of desolation hit me.

Just a girl on a bench.

I laughed at that thought, sniffling and wiping my face with my arm. Yeah, just a girl—with a psychotic Greek goddess after her ass, a curse hanging over her head, and a father and a friend to rescue. . . .

After a while I pressed my palms against my eyelids, swallowing the worries and forcing the grief away with controlled inhales and exhales.

"First days don't always go so well, do they?"

I lifted my hand and squinted. Michel Lamarliere, my legal guardian for the next six months, until I turned eighteen, stood in the grass regarding me with a kind expression in his gray eyes, his hands clasped behind his back. The guy had presence, an air about him that anyone with half a brain could sense. Power and knowledge seemed to cling to him. The swirling tattoo that wound up the side of his neck, ear, and temple only added to his image.

He definitely fit his role as one of the nine Novem heads and leader of the Lamarliere family of witches. Michel was something of a rarity in his world; power was usually passed down maternally in witch families, but every once in a while it passed to a male—Michel being one of them. Sebastian, his son, being another . . .

It was hard to look at Michel and not see Sebastian in the raven hair and stormy gray eyes. Even harder not to feel the uncomfortable mix of confusion and regret. Since Violet's disappearance, Sebastian and I hadn't really spoken at all. And after he'd seen firsthand what I'd eventually become . . . well, I was pretty sure whatever interest there might've been evaporated in an instant.

I sat up, removed my feet from the bench arm, and wiped my face. "I'm not sure any time in The Dungeon goes well, first day or not."

"Ah. The Dungeon. That certainly explains things." He gestured to the bench. "May I?"

I shrugged and slid over. "If you don't mind the stench."

"No one spends time training with Bran without working up a sweat. I take it he was rather hard on you." Michel sat down.

"'Brutal' is probably a better word." I stared at the grass. "He doesn't waste any time, does he?"

"He does his job extremely well. 'Failure' is not in his vocabulary or in his heart. If your goal is to learn and learn quickly, then you have no better teacher on your side. Unless, of course, you count me. And since you ditched my class, you have no evidence but my word."

I glanced at him and winced, realizing that the last class I skipped by coming out here was Michel's. "Sorry."

He tipped his face to the sky and closed his eyes. "It was an excuse to leave the confines of my classroom and enjoy the sunlight." Since Michael had been a prisoner of Athena's for a decade, I could see why he'd take any opportunity he could to be outside. "My teaching assistant needed time with the students anyway. Tomorrow I'll see about switching your classes around. Bran's should be the last class of the day."

"Thanks." Being able to bolt straight from The Dungeon would be nice. Though spending the entire school day dreading

Bran's class—not so nice. "So what's his deal, anyway? I mean, I know he's head of the Ramsey family and everything. . . ."

Michel straightened a bit and shifted his angle on the bench to face me better. "Some history in lieu of class, then. As I'm sure you already know, Bran is a demigod. The Ramseys are the descendants of Celtic gods and their human consorts. Bran is the great-grandson of the late war god Camulus, on his paternal side. Being a direct descendant makes him head of the family, which is quite large. Strengths, weaknesses, traits—they all run differently through each individual just as in any family tree. . . . Bran is blessed with many attributes from his godly ancestor."

I snorted. "I can only imagine."

"Not surprising he has a war god in his family tree, no?" Michel said with a small laugh. "Bran possesses great strength, speed, and agility, and a long life. He is a warrior at heart, a true chip off the old block, if you will."

I shook my head in disbelief, thinking back on my old life, one that seemed so far away now even though I'd only been in New 2 for a short time. I never could've imagined that so much truth and unknown facts lay within myths and legends. Or that I was part of those myths.

But the reality of the supernatural wasn't as surprising to me as it probably would've been to someone else outside of The Rim. Even as a kid I knew the paranormal existed, because I'd grown up with it, had witnessed it time and time again when I'd cut or dye my hair and it'd be back to the same length and color when I awoke the next day. The way my blue-green eyes were brighter than they should be. . . .

During the nights and slow hours, I let my mind wander and I processed the truth, as crazy as it was. But really, what other option did I have but to put one foot in front of the other? I wasn't the type to give in to hysterics. The pain and abuse I'd suffered as a child—those experiences shaped me, made me able to handle everything I'd faced since. If I could deal with *that* and come out with my mind intact, I could deal with any paranormal shit that came my way.

"'Demigod,'" Michel continued, "is perhaps not the correct term since there are no true half god, half humans left, to our knowledge, but we have used the term for so long that now it encompasses any descendant of the gods."

"So why are demigods and shape-shifters lumped together when people refer to the Novem families?" I asked. The Novem consisted of three vampire families, three witch families, and three demigod/shape-shifter families. There were other families out there, but these nine were the ones who'd had the money and power to come together and buy New Orleans all those years ago.

"Oftentimes the words 'shape-shifter' and 'demigod' are interchangeable, as the ability to change forms is one of the gifts that can be passed down through a godly ancestor." His eyebrow arched. "You would be learning some of this in my class had you come."

I glanced over and shrugged, smiling. "Are they immortal? Is Bran?"

Michel shook his head. "No one is truly immortal, Ari. Long-lived, certainly, but even the gods can be killed. By rival gods or by"—he looked at me—"a god-killer like you. True immortality is, perhaps, mere myth."

I laughed. All this *was* myth. Everything I'd learned about New 2 and the Novem, all of it was like jumping into the pages of *Bulfinch's Mythology*. I rubbed both hands down my face.

"Feeling a bit like Alice in Wonderland, I imagine?"

I sat back and stretched my legs out in front of me. "You have no idea."

"Go home; get some rest. My family has seen to placing wards—protection spells—around that crumbling mansion you call a home, though I wish you would reconsider my offer. . . ."

"I like the GD and my crumbling home."

He frowned, shaking his head like he couldn't comprehend it. "My son says the same. Keep watch. Be on guard. You have your blade," he said, nodding to the τέρας blade strapped to my thigh. "And you have those assigned to shadow you."

That was news to me. "What do you mean?"

"Protection. You won't see them or hear them, but they will be there, guarding you. And that is not up for argument. Athena's plan for you is unclear. I suspect she is giving you time to squirm, to worry over your friend and your father, and break you down mentally, but one never knows with her. Better to have you protected at all times."

He patted my knee and got up. "Go home, Ari. Rest. Eat. Tomorrow will be another brutal day at Presby, I'm sure."

I rolled my eyes but gave him a parting smile, which faded slowly, along with his image, as my thoughts sobered. Nothing would be as brutal as facing Athena again. Presby was going to be a breeze compared to that.

Everyone knows what you are now. Bran's words echoed in my head.

The constant knocking rhythm of the streetcar on its tracks lulled me into a thoughtful state. I stared out the window as the car took me up St. Charles Avenue and into the Garden District.

From the moment I stopped in front of the Presbytère building this morning and watched the students hurrying inside, I noticed the quick glances, the recognition. They whispered in the halls, cast glances in study hall, in the cafeteria, but it wasn't just the snow white hair or the unnatural-looking teal light to my eyes.

It wasn't that at all.

Outward appearances no longer mattered so much. They had mattered a great deal beyond The Rim, where anything unusual set you apart, but here in New 2, the shocking thing was on the inside, not the outside. And apparently word spread fast.

I guess after the battle with Athena, there was no hiding what I was.

I'd once told Violet to never change.

You shouldn't either, you know, she'd told me in that strange, insightful way of hers.

And yet I had this need, this terrible, burning need to be accepted, to be seen as normal. My old social services counselor would say it was because of my abandonment, my childhood, and knocking around from one home to another. I knew that I was broken and missing some parts. I knew I had issues. I even knew all the proper things I was supposed to do to make a Better Me, but knowing and getting that *something* inside you to work right again? Yeah. Hadn't figured that one out yet.

The streetcar slowed. I hurried to pull on my hoodie; the sweat from my workout had dried cold on my skin.

The sun was just beginning its descent below the horizon, washing the street in hazy gold. I stepped off the car and crossed St. Charles, noticing that a few more houses along the street were occupied, no doubt restored by the Novem and rented out to Mardi Gras revelers who still came to New 2 in droves.

It was the season, after all.

But otherwise, the Novem had yet to lay claim to the GD. Eventually they'd work their way in and start restoring houses, taking over, and leaving the orphans and independent *doué* (us non-Novem folks with abilities) homeless.

My boots crunched over the ruined sidewalk as I made my way down Washington Avenue. Leaving St. Charles Avenue and entering any of the side streets was like stepping into another world, a shadowy, wild, forgotten place where tall houses stood and trees and vines blocked out the sun.

Gardens were overgrown, tangles of Spanish moss and vines thrived and grew unchecked, mansions were abandoned and rotting but still elegant and dominating. . . . It was, to me, the most beautiful place on earth.

Old oaks leaned over both sides of the street, their twisted limbs reaching and tangling and creating a dark, eerie tunnel. Random shafts of golden haze pierced through the thick canopy, turning Washington Avenue into a forest of gossamer saplings.

I walked a meandering path down the middle of the street,

in and out of light and shadow, until I closed in on my destination: Lafayette Cemetery.

Lafayette *Swamp* Cemetery.

City of the Dead.

Land of the Creepy Crawlies.

THREE

THE MUSTY TANG OF DEAD LEAVES AND WET GROUND BECAME so strong I could taste the damp, decaying atmosphere in the back of my throat.

The massive arched gate loomed in front of me. It would've read LAFAYETTE CEMETERY NO. 1, if it hadn't been covered in vines. One side of the gate hung open in invitation. I stopped in the street. I hadn't been here since Violet had disappeared.

For a long time I stared at the open gate, at the tombs beyond and the crumbled wall that used to surround the cemetery. Some time after the hurricanes—the Twin Sisters, people around here called them—a tall iron fence had been erected around the property, holding in the rubble and what remained of the original cemetery wall.

I wasn't sure if it was meant to keep people out or to keep other things in.

I bit the inside of my cheek, working up the nerve to go inside and, at the same time, trying to put a lid on the anxiety this place gave me. There were a lot of fresh memories here. Bad ones. I squared my shoulders anyway and went through the gate, ducking beneath the vines.

The once-paved avenue that stretched out in front of me was littered with cracked concrete, mossy bones, and years of debris and leaves. It was flanked by aboveground tombs and vaults, some taller than me by several feet and still intact. Others were nothing but rubble.

This was the place where I'd faced Athena, where I'd inhaled the ground-up toe bone of Alice Cromley, the infamous Creole clairvoyant. Her remains had shown me the truth of my curse and the horror my ancestor, Medusa, had gone through.

I passed the spot where Daniel, Josephine Arnaud's assistant, had been killed in the battle with Athena. A slash of cloth waved from a small branch, snagged there during the fight, probably. Signs of the battle were everywhere in the disturbed leaves, the dried blood splattered on marble. . . .

My gaze fixed on the low, twisted tree limb where Athena had once sat and the tomb where she'd delivered a heart-stopping show with me as the star. I stopped as the mental image of

Athena flashed before my eyes, the demented sociopathic goddess of war, sitting on the peak of that cracked marble tomb, her feet dangling over the edge.

"How about we just show them instead? A little taste . . . a vision . . . just enough to show you, *dear Ari, that you don't belong . . ."*

Brutality and arrogance shone in her eyes as greenish bolts of power shot from her hands to lift me off the damp ground. I hovered as though floating in water, my hair coming loose and spreading out in white waves.

And then the pain. My scalp burning. My heart hammering out of control. Fear, primal and raw, as things began moving and splitting my scalp, rising up in writhing, milky, serpentlike shadows—a sickening, terrifying vision of what was to come.

My friends had gaped at me in horror. It was exactly what Athena had wanted. My place was with her, she'd said. And Sebastian could never, *ever* be interested in someone like me. My eyelids slid closed as I mentally dulled the sharp truth of that memory.

Then I resumed my walk, letting thoughts of Sebastian finally filter in as I searched the cemetery. The short time we'd spent together had been spontaneous and crazy, a middle finger to a messed-up world, a messed-up life. Escapism at its finest.

I was well aware of why, when I'd woken in Sebastian's arms

and our gazes locked, I'd taken a chance and let things happen.

It was called loneliness. Maybe a little desperation, too. And it felt right. Normal.

I was in a city alone, freaked out by what I'd learned about my mother and even more freaked out about the hunter I'd killed. And there was Sebastian. He saw me. *Me*. Being the empath that he was, I suppose he'd sensed a lot of things that day. Both different. Both loners. And maybe that had allowed him to see past all the barriers too, and just go with the moment.

I sighed. I had no idea how he felt now or where we stood. Athena had showed him and the others what I'd become, and he'd stepped back, pale with shock. Stupid me for being drawn to the possibility of an "us" like a moth to a flame. He'd fled, and even though he'd come back with reinforcements, it didn't mean he was still interested. How could he be when he saw what I was? How could anyone be okay with that?

There was only one person who hadn't run away that day in the cemetery. Violet.

My throat thickened and my eyes stung. I hunched my shoulders and picked up my pace.

That tiny, pale, Gothic child with her black bob, dark eyes, pert nose, and eerie fangs had pushed her Mardi Gras mask onto the top of her head and stared at me in wonder.

Fucking *wonder*.

I sniffed back angry tears, swiping my sleeve across my nose.

In the end, they'd returned—Dub, Crank, Henri, and Sebastian. They'd accepted me despite knowing what lurked, even now, inside me. But there had been nothing in the world like Violet's complete and utter acceptance.

Violet had launched her little body at Athena and stabbed the goddess of war in the heart. And then they'd vanished, Violet still clinging to Athena.

That strange little girl had tried to protect me, and I'd do anything in my power to get her back.

Anything.

Which brought me back to the task at hand. I climbed over a large debris pile of marble, bones, funerary boxes, and urns, paying close attention to where my boots landed. At the top I balanced and then scanned the far end of the cemetery.

Cypress tress grew at the south end where the land had sunk, allowing stagnant water to form a small brackish swamp right in the middle of the GD, and making it so humid that a damp film covered everything.

Tombs poked through the shallow black water along with the short knobby knees of the cypress trees, and Spanish moss hung in long lacy tendrils from the branches above.

A flash of white caught my attention. But it was just a crane, shaking its feathers.

I slid down the pile and approached the edge of the swamp. With each step my boots sank deeper into the soft earth.

Somewhere in that dark, shaded swamp was Violet's white alligator, I hoped. The cemetery had been the last place any of us had seen him.

I called his name even though I felt like an idiot. Startled, the crane took flight, things moved and shuffled in the branches, and the water rippled.

I waited. And then . . . nothing.

I needed to find Pascal, to do something for Violet until I found the means to save her. And I just prayed he hadn't waddled off to parts unknown.

The last bit of daylight was fading fast, so I made my way down the row of tombs and then up the east side, back toward the gate. Disappointment sat heavy on my shoulders as I crossed the dark street and made for the rotting mansion I now called home.

Four

As I walked the four blocks down Coliseum Street to First Street, the last bit of light gave way to darkness. No streetlamps. No traffic. Only the occupied mansions were illuminated, lit from behind grimy windowpanes. It made them seem warm and alive, watching within a sea of blackness. Walking in the GD at night wasn't for the fainthearted.

My gaze went up as it always did when I looked at my new home. The two-story Italianate mansion dominated the corner with its double porches wrapped in iron railings. The mauve paint was faded and chipped. The tall black shutters still framed the windows, though some hung lopsided, barely clinging on.

A content feeling came over me as I stepped onto the sidewalk.

The lawn was overgrown, the fence around the house barely visible beneath mounds of wild vines, but the place had character—the neglected, soulful, earthy kind. This was my home along with Crank, Henri, Dub, Violet, and Sebastian. Some would call us squatters, misfits, the fringe of Novem society. It was all true.

The scent of hot spices leaked from the house. I opened the front door and entered the large foyer with its wide, sweeping staircase and the massive iron chandelier hanging above. The Crypt, the Gothic-looking dining room, was to my right and the living room to my left.

The wood in the house was rotting in the damp, humid climate. The expensive wallpaper had all but peeled away. The plasterwork was cracked and tiny bits fell randomly or whenever one of us slammed a door. 1331 First Street reminded me of a once-wealthy southern belle who was now flat broke and refusing to admit it.

My stomach growled. Voices drifted from the living room, so I followed the sound.

Dub was on the floor picking through a pile of stolen grave goods dumped onto the coffee table. Crank sat in one of the chairs across from the couch in her usual cabbie hat, braids, and grease-stained overalls.

Sebastian's forearms rested on his knees as he leaned forward and spoke to Dub from the love seat, but at my entry, he went silent and lifted his head. The gray-eyed stare shot right to my stomach and made it weightless. Sebastian's eyes were the color of smoke and silver. His pale skin, raven hair, and naturally dark red lips, paired with a rebel attitude and a poet's soul, pulled me in like a dark, magnetic force.

Crank had told me that Sebastian could feel what others felt. And when he looked at me, it sure as hell felt like he could see past all the bullshit and right into the very heart of who I was. All my secrets, all my fears, hopes, dreams, beliefs—all those things I'd never allow others to know.

Footsteps echoed over the hardwood floor behind me. I broke eye contact with Sebastian as Henri angled by with a large stainless steel pot. I followed him to the coffee table, where he set the pot next to Dub's loot. A stack of plastic bowls hung from his crooked finger, and there were silver spoons in his grip.

"How was Presby?" Crank asked.

I let my bag slide to the floor and plopped down on one end of the couch as Henri took a seat on the other end. "Tiring."

Crank snorted. "And you were trying to talk us into going. Crazy talk, Ari. Crazy talk."

Well, I guessed I couldn't really argue the point anymore. Presby was stuffy, arrogant, and totally out of my league, so I could just imagine the experience Crank and Dub would have there. They might not be well educated, but I'd like to see a twelve-year-old Novem kid fix a motor, work for a living, and feed themselves on ingenuity alone.

My stomach growled again.

"Here." Henri shoved a bowl full of red beans and rice my way. *"Bon appétit."*

"*Merci,*" I said, using one of a few French words I knew. The food was hot in temperature and in taste, and extremely good. "More stuff for Spits?" I asked Dub after several bites, gesturing to the pile of grave goods on the table.

"Yeah." He scratched beneath his short blond Afro and a frown appeared, creasing the light brown skin of his forehead. "Not the best take ever. Guess he can melt down some of these gold teeth. Few pieces of jewelry . . . I'll need to go out again first thing tomorrow."

Spits was a guy in the Quarter who bought the things Dub scavenged in the cemeteries. He cleaned the sellable items and then resold them to tourists in his antique shop, and the tourists didn't have a clue they were buying and wearing stuff taken off dead people.

"Why the rush?" I asked.

He raised his grass-green eyes. "Mardi Gras. The tourists are here in droves. Spits is buying. They spend money, so . . ." He pulled something from his pocket and tossed it over the table.

A piece of metal hit me in the chest and landed in my lap. "What's this?"

"Thought you'd like it." Dub shrugged and went back to his sorting.

I picked the ring off my lap with two fingers.

"It's got a crescent moon on it," Crank explained. "Like your tattoo."

I touched the small black crescent moon tattooed on my right cheekbone. I also wore a platinum moon on a black ribbon around my neck. New Orleans was once called the Crescent City, and I'd long ago adopted the symbol as my own because it reminded me of my mother, and the place I was born.

I held the ring out to him, trying not to let it gross me out. "Well, thanks for the thought, but I kind of draw the line at wearing something pulled off a dead person."

"Says the girl who inhaled Alice Cromley's toe bone," Henri muttered with his mouth full.

I shot him a smirk. "It was a bit of ground-up bone; it's not like I sucked down a whole toe." As I looked away I caught Sebastian's small smile. He shook his head at Henri and then resumed eating.

"Relax. I got the ring from a house in Audubon Place," Dub told me. "You know, the big white one on the corner."

"He found it helping me clear the house of rats and snakes,"

Henri said. "Some of the Novem families are moving back into those behemoths. I think some of them used to live there. But you watch. They'll be coming into the GD next, and then we'll all be screwed and have to live in the ruins." A string of what I could only guess were French curses flowed under his breath.

I rolled the ring around in my hand. It was heavy, made of silver and inset with a pale crescent moon cut from some kind of pale bluish stone. "I like it. Thanks, Dub." The ring fit on the middle finger of my left hand. I left it there and finished eating.

Henri cast a glare at Dub, his irises flashing that odd hazel-yellow color. "We were *supposed* to leave the contents alone. You'd better hope the Novem doesn't have any records of what was in that safe in the closet, or I'm out of a job. And if I am"—he pointed his spoon—"you and me are gonna go round."

Dub rolled his eyes, let out a disbelieving snort, and grabbed a bowl.

While I wasn't originally a fan of Henri's bossy attitude, once I got used to his surliness, he was an okay guy and he had a gruffness about him that I liked. *He could definitely use a shave and a haircut,* I thought. And those eyes of his were sleek and arresting, like a predator's. . . .

"This isn't half bad, Henri," Crank managed through a mouthful of rice and beans.

"Wait till you see the mess I left in the kitchen." Henri

propped his feet on the corner of the table, looking pretty damn pleased with himself. "I cook. The infants clean."

Dub's narrowing eyes lifted as he dropped the spoon into his bowl, a look of pure irritation on his face. "You suck, Henri. You don't have to make such a big mess every time. We know you do it on purpose." He flopped back, bracing against the chair behind him and dragging his bowl with him.

"Yeah," Crank muttered. "Tell me about it."

Henri chuckled and took a bite of his food—happy now that he'd annoyed the young ones in true big-brother fashion.

After we ate, I helped clean up the chaos in the kitchen. Dub and Crank chattered nonstop as Sebastian and I worked silently. Every once in a while he'd smile at something they said or shake his head. His mood seemed way better than it had when Violet first disappeared.

Once the kitchen was decent, I went upstairs to my room on the second floor, where a small fire already burned in the marble fireplace.

Probably Dub, I thought as I shed my blades and then clothes.

The great thing about the old mansions? En suite bathrooms. And though no one drank the water without boiling it, we were able to shower and use the toilet. The main water lines were working, and so as long as the pipes coming into and out of the house were undamaged, water was available.

I showered, noticing a few light bruises—courtesy of Bran—and then dressed in pajama pants and a T-shirt. After twisting my wet hair into a knot, I settled onto my sleeping bag.

"I can get you a mattress for the bed, now that you're staying," Crank said, peeking around the doorway.

"The sleeping bag is fine. Don't trouble yourself."

"It's no trouble. If I come across one, I'll snag it for you."

I smiled. "Okay, thanks."

I lay down, the room dark except for the fire, tucked my hands behind my head, and watched the shadows dance over the plaster medallion on the ceiling, wondering how my next day at Presby would play out.

Five

"Our newest student at Presby brings attention to an important subject . . ."

Oh great, not another one.

I let my forehead fall onto the top of my desk with a loud thunk. I'd been singled out all day by teachers in nearly every class. I guess yesterday, being my first day, they'd all given me a break (all but Bran), but today, apparently, I was fair game.

". . . and while I intended to cover the Wars of the Pantheons later in the semester, I think perhaps now is a better-suited time, especially in light of recent events. Today we'll discuss Athena. She is, after all, our enemy, one we'd be wise to study. So, who can tell me about her?"

Mrs. Cromley, of the Novem's Cromley family of witches,

presumably, and professor of history, leaned her slim hip against the desk and folded her arms over her chest. She was in her early forties, maybe. Pretty. Had that really intellectual look about her.

Someone spoke up behind me. "Athena was the Greek goddess of wisdom, warfare, strategy . . . um . . ."

When silence reigned, Cromley encouraged the rest of the class, "Chime in. Anyone."

"Justice."

"Strength?"

The room went quiet again, so the professor finished. "She was the goddess of the arts, agriculture, crafts like weaving and metalworking, skills, culture. . . . Athena was, and still is, intensely interested in culture and civilization. She prided herself on being a part of not only Greek civilization but every subsequent civilization thereafter. If you think she speaks only Greek, ignores mankind, and walks around carrying an olive branch, think again." A few students chuckled at that.

Cromley pushed away from her desk and walked slowly back and forth. "Since we are her enemies, it's safe to say she knows everything there is to know about us. How we think, the things that are important to us, what we eat, how we talk, our modern weapons and technology. This is no stuck-in-the-ancient-past goddess. Her art is strategy, and she didn't get to where she is now by being stupid or too lofty to immerse herself in our way of life. Athena is cunning, highly intelligent, and powerful. She was a champion of heroes and mankind until"—she stopped moving and paused for effect—"sometime in the tenth century, when she killed Zeus and took over his temple, and the War of the Pantheons began. Can anyone tell me why she did this?"

Interested, I glanced around the room. Most of the students were older than I was by a year or two, this being a college-level course, and yet none of them seemed to know the answer.

"The truth is," Cromley finally said, "no one knows. No one knows what caused the rift. Only that it was swift, brutal, and absolute. Some say it was a power struggle long in the making; some say it was a betrayal. Some say that time has a way of reshaping the gods, slowly turning them from good to bad and back again over thousands of years. Cycling through personalities, if you will.

"It was during this long war that Athena began turning our ancestors into what we call τέρας, the Greek word for 'monster.' In fact, it is known that she made an entire army of minions to aid in her cause in the war, many of whom were killed in the battles. She targeted mostly vampires, witches, shape-shifters, and demigods because their natural abilities allowed her to make τέρας of great power. She took witches and made them into harpies. She used shape-shifters to create all manner of monsters. She kidnapped demigods to form into her immortal hunters. And she used humans as well. All this, as you can imagine, led to our banding together and taking a stand against Athena. And when some of her own τέρας turned against her and joined us, we have been on her 'Annihilate' list ever since."

The ancestors Cromley spoke of had branched off the human evolutionary tree a *long* time ago and evolved into humans of a different kind. Vampires, witches, monsters . . . And I'd learned during my short time in Athena's prison that the prisoners had three classifications: Borns, beings born of power, such as vampires, witches, and shape-shifters. Mades, beings made or turned into something grotesque by The Bitch herself. And then there were the Beauties, those of rare beauty who simply inspired jealousy. Beauties would become Made at some point to satisfy Athena's ego. Medusa had been a Beauty.

In the darkness of Athena's prison I'd been asked if I was a Beauty. The thought made me snort, because take away the hair and eyes, and I was left with an average face. Not ugly. Not gorgeous. Just normal.

"Ari."

I blinked. "Huh?"

Cromley frowned at me. "I was informing the class about your ancestors. The gorgons."

"Oh . . . ," I said slowly, looking around and wondering what she wanted me to say about it. *Um, yeah, it totally sucks being cursed and knowing one day you'll become a disgusting snake-headed monster.*

Athena had hunted each of my female ancestors, and for what? For being what *she* created them to be? Because she was afraid of the power she'd mistakenly given them? Just the thought of it made my blood boil and my hands ball into tight fists.

Cromley decided to continue her lecture without my input, which was good because I wasn't sure I could speak at that moment.

Athena had cursed the once-beautiful and devout Medusa and made her into a gorgon, all because some shithead of a god raped Medusa on the floor of Athena's pristine seaside temple. Had Athena blamed the god? Hell, no. The goddess of *justice* had blamed Medusa and cursed my ancestor's beauty so that it became something so hideous that just one glance at her face would turn another to stone.

Only, Athena had forgotten to exempt the gods from Medusa's power.

The goddess of wisdom had created a god-killer.

And once she'd realized that, she'd charged Perseus with killing her creation, which he did. But what neither of them had counted on was Medusa's child, who had been hidden away—a child who was cursed like her mother to have strange eyes and hair the color of moonlight, a child who would follow in her mother's footsteps and become a monster in her twenty-first year, the same age Medusa had been when she was cursed.

And so it began, from mother to daughter, all the way down to me.

And according to the curse, I had less than four years left.

Sometime before my twenty-first year, I was destined to birth a daughter, be hunted by the Sons of Perseus, and either commit suicide like my mother, be killed, or turn into the monster I feared most.

But I wasn't like all the others before me.

I was the daughter of a gorgon, true. But my father was a Son of Perseus, a hunter who tracked down and destroyed Athena's monstrous creations. τέρας hunters. This had apparently made me into a different kind of freak, one who didn't need to "mature" at twenty-one or become a monster in order to turn people to stone. I could do it now with a touch. *Not that I'm any good at it.*

But I was trying. Violet was counting on me. My father, who had betrayed Athena by falling in love with my mother instead of killing her, was counting on me. Christ, even now Athena was probably torturing them. I gripped the edge of the desk hard, my fear and imagination running wild as Cromley continued to talk about Athena.

"The ancient myths the world knows speak of Athena's goodness, her just ways, her support of mankind and the heroes she chose to aid. But even in those, you will find that for all her good deeds, there are just as many bad. She was vicious in her unfairness to Medusa. She blinded Tiresias simply because he stumbled upon her bathing. She was given to fits of rage, jealousy, and unthinkable acts even in ancient times. And now she is known for the horrors she inflicts upon innocents, the sadistic mind games, the brutality, the torture. . . ."

Abruptly, I stood up, my chair scraping across the floor, my heart racing. Cromley stopped talking. I was out the door with my backpack and down the hall before she could even ask me what was wrong.

What was *wrong* was that the professor's words made me sick to my stomach. With Violet and my father in Athena's clutches, the last thing I wanted to hear was how horrible Athena was. I already knew it. I could imagine plenty what they were going through, and I sure as hell didn't need to hear it from someone else.

I ducked into the girls' bathroom, leaned back against the door, and tried to catch my breath. I stepped to the sink and splashed cold water on my face, then gazed at myself in the mirror.

What was I doing? How could I think for one second that I could beat Athena? I wasn't even a David to her Goliath; I was more like an ant facing Mount Everest.

Yet I had to do something. And Violet. God, she was just a kid, only eight years old. Her age wouldn't make a difference to Athena; she'd hurt her anyway.

Nausea mushroomed like a noxious cloud in my gut. I swallowed, my mouth watering in a sick way.

Oh God.

I grabbed my stomach, darted into an open stall, and puked.

My palms were damp as I braced my hands against the walls of the bathroom stall. I stayed there catching my breath and allowing my rapid pulse to return to normal.

The bathroom door opened. Soft footsteps shuffled against the tile. I flushed the toilet and walked out, sidestepping a young girl and heading to the sink to rinse out my mouth and splash more water on my face.

After drying off with a paper towel, I unbound my hair and shook it out, breathing in deeply and trying to rid myself of the queasiness that still lingered.

I reached up to make a braid at each temple, which I'd pull back into a tight knot with the rest of my hair. It kept the front strands from loosening out of my knot and getting in my eyes when I was training.

I'd only managed to gather a strip and part it into thirds when I saw the girl's small face staring at me in the mirror's reflection. She was young like Violet, with loose brown hair and brown eyes. She was dressed like everyone else in Presby: black pants or skirt and white collared shirt. Well, everyone but me; I'd come to Presby this morning in black from head to toe.

I narrowed my eyes at her through the mirror. "What?"

"Is it real?" she squeaked out, eyes big and round.

"My hair?" She nodded. "Yeah, it's real."

I'd hated my hair for so long that it was difficult to see it in the same light as other people—a thick, glossy sheet of white that reached the small of my back. I'd hated it for the sole reason that it attracted attention, and when you're a kid being passed from one foster parent to the next, sometimes hiding and *not* being noticed is the difference between—

I clamped down on my thoughts and gave the girl a wry smile in the mirror, resuming my task with the idea that all the crap that had happened to me when I was young probably would have happened regardless of my hair. Maybe all it took to be mistreated was the fact that I was there, available, and defenseless.

"Is it true? Are you really a god-killer?" the girl asked in a small, scared voice.

I finished with the braid and moved to the other side. I knew what drove her to ask. The entire student body was probably terrified I'd break out the scales and turn them all to stone. I didn't like being the center of attention, and I definitely didn't like it when the reason was fear.

Feeling awkward but wanting to set her mind at ease, I said the only dumb thing that came to mind. "I am. And I only use my powers for good." I nodded toward a stall as my cheeks went warm. "You'd better go if you're gonna go."

She blinked, snapping to attention, and then darted into one of the stalls. My reflection rolled its eyes at the line I'd fed her. It was more complicated than that. I planned on using my power for vigilante justice, for vengeance, and I wasn't so sure whether that would put me in the "good" category or not.

After finishing with the braids, I gathered them with the rest of my hair, twisted a tight bun, and secured it with the plain black band from around my wrist. And then I went into the handicapped stall to change.

Six

"You're early."

I let the door to The Dungeon bang closed behind me and gave Bran a shrug. "I'm ready to train." And I'd rather be worked into the ground than feel the sheer despair and helplessness I'd felt moments earlier in the bathroom. A good workout always helped put me back on track, even if it did come with a few bumps and bruises.

I dropped my bag by the door, went to the center of the room, and sat down to stretch. It took less than a minute for Bran's shadow to fall over me. I glanced up. He crossed his arms over his chest and stared down at me with a gruff expression. "At least you're wearing appropriate clothes this time."

"Brought them with me." The loose cargo pants and sport

tank were oldies, but the most comfortable training gear I had.

"Get up."

I got to my feet, cracked my knuckles, and gave him a cocky smile that I knew he'd appreciate. "Ready to have your ass handed to you, Ramsey?"

A slow grin split his face. "Bring it on, Snow White."

"Snow White has black hair. Know your Disney movies."

And so began thirty minutes of relentless physical training. Bran wanted me prepared to fend off any kind of attack, and I couldn't exactly use my power if I couldn't keep Athena's minions or hunters from killing me first. It was all part of the training, he said. Blocks, kicks, punches. Offense. Defense. Learning to bend my enemy's body parts in new ways that would stop them in their tracks.

Then came the blade training.

I was to the point where I could barely breathe, and my hand, wrist, and forearm burned with exertion and the constant vibration of steel meeting steel. Bran tossed his training blade behind him. It slid across the floor and hit the wall. He grabbed my shoulder with one hand and slugged me hard in the gut with the other.

I doubled over, dropping my blade, straining and gasping for air that wouldn't come.

"NOW! RIGHT NOW!" He circled around me, intensity

coming off him in heavy waves. "Use that shock, that one-second burst of fear! Tap into it at *that* moment when there is only reaction, then fling your energy, your emotions, back out. Your power will come with it. Don't think about it; just do it."

I raised a hand in surrender, still doubled over, unable to speak, the pain spreading through my torso in a severe cramp-style ache.

He continued circling. I knew he was coming in for another hit. *Suck it up! If you can't handle him, you can't handle whatever Athena will throw at you!* Tears blurred my vision, but I blinked them back and straightened.

And then I blocked.

"Use your power!"

We went round and round like that for what seemed like hours. I kept trying to use my power, to make something happen, but failed at every turn.

"Stop holding it in!" he yelled at me. "Stop relying solely on your physical defenses!"

Punch. Block. Jab. I couldn't help it. I was human; this was what I knew how to do.

"When pain hits you, you strike back! You're too in control, that's your problem. Your ability to take the pain, swallow it, and stay focused is the problem."

I dropped my defensive stance and let my arms fall limp at

my sides. "What the hell kind of fighting is that?" I said irritably, trying to catch my breath at the same time. "That's the first thing they teach you: Stay calm and focused. Now you're telling me not to?"

He stopped moving and put his hands on his hips. "Yeah, that's what I'm telling you, Selkirk. Even a baby could understand what I'm saying. I've got to break you down before I can build you back up. Fear and adrenaline are what stir your power. You have to get used to the feel of it, let it pass that damn wall of yours, and *then* we can work on focus and control." He moved again.

A blur to my left. I saw it coming and blocked his first swing with my forearm, dropping down and spinning in anticipation of the next hit. But he came at me with a boot to the side of my knee.

I cried out with a sharp curse, my entire body dipping toward the pain. And yeah, it was there, that instant burst of shock, like a gasp of the heart. The moment Bran had been talking about.

I grabbed his ankle. Like a slingshot, the fear and adrenaline whipped through me and then back out through my grip. *Strike.* In an instant I felt the power surge out of me, snapping like an electrical current, so quick and terrifying that I released Bran and fell back, eyes wide and panting.

Holy cow.

My hand was numb. I was trembling so hard that I couldn't even sit up straight, so instead I balanced myself with my palms flat on the floor. This had been the goal, but, goddamn, it scared the shit out of me.

Bran sat a few feet away from me, pant leg rolled up, eyeing his ankle and calf, the skin nearly white. After a few seconds he released his leg and shot me a triumphant grin. "Better."

He pushed to his feet and held out a hand to me. I took it and let him pull me up. "Again tomorrow," he said, dismissing me, and then walked to his table for a drink.

That was all the praise I got? *Better.* I shook my head, smiling despite the aches and pains, because as tough as Bran acted, he was a good guy. And in the last fifty minutes he'd taught me things with a blade and my body that I never knew were possible.

I went to my bag, grabbed the bottled water I'd gotten from the cafeteria earlier, and downed most of it. Then I sheathed my blade, pulled on my jacket, and left the room.

My thoughts turned to Athena. With my training started, my other objective was to get inside her head, figure out her weaknesses and where she might have taken Violet.

And for that, I needed Michel's help.

The Lamarliere House was in the French Quarter, so I didn't have too far to walk from Presby, down St. Peter Street to Royal, where Michel's three-story house loomed on the corner.

My legs were still weak and shaky, and the sweat on my skin was starting to dry, leaving me feeling cold. Already the aches and pains from my training were settling in. Tomorrow the soreness would be almost unbearable. I made a mental note to stop at the drugstore near Canal Street and grab some Advil on my way home.

The "before dinner" crowd had yet to trickle into the streets, but there was still activity, still music drifting from open doors, tourists shopping, and the clip-clop of hooves on asphalt.

I breathed in deeply, loving the scent of sun-warmed bricks and all the different aromas from the bakeries and restaurants.

In the thirteen years since the Novem bought the ruined city, the Quarter had been completely restored. It was now a very expensive tourist destination, carefully overseen by the Novem and one of their biggest sources of income, one that swelled during Mardi Gras. Once the sun went down, another parade would start and the sidewalks would be crammed with people.

I noticed a few looks and frowns thrown my way as I headed toward the enormous house on the corner, pretty sure it had something to do with the blade sheathed at my side. No doubt to them I was just another strange kid in New 2 with dyed white hair, combat boots, and a fake short sword strapped to her thigh.

If only they knew the truth.

I smiled at the tourists I passed, hopped onto the sidewalk, and rang the bell. The door opened. The butler took one look at me, let me inside, and then led me to the second floor, the main living area of the house.

I'd only been here once, after escaping Athena's prison. I'd heard the Novem heads talking about me in Michel's library like I was some sort of weapon to be used or gotten rid of—*not* a pleasant memory—and I'd fled to the GD.

I waited as the butler opened the tall French doors leading outside. Ferns hung between the wrought-iron framework that supported the courtyard balcony, and at each end, steps curved down to the ground below.

I took vague note of the large patio and a rectangular yard of green grass, which led into a pretty English-style garden complete with a pool and a small cottage/pool house. But the grandeur of Michel's courtyard took second stage.

Sebastian was standing in the center of the yard.

My hands curled slowly around the iron railing as I stared at his profile. I wished like hell the chaos I felt inside would go away. It was there every time I saw him—excitement, anxiety, warmth, happiness, worry. . . .

The butler left me there, returning inside and closing the doors.

Michel stood in front of Sebastian, about ten feet away, and spoke in low, muted tones. I watched, stunned, as a ball of sheer blue light formed over Sebastian's outstretched hand. It was the size of a soccer ball. He played with it, moving his hand up, over, and away from it as it hovered in front of him.

Michel's calm, instructional voice continued. I strained to hear his words.

Sebastian lifted the orb over his head and passed it from one hand to the other, then brought it back down and placed it in front of himself at chest level. His movements looked graceful, like tai chi, controlled as though he was pulling . . . something . . . from the air, the earth, shaping the light. Only the ball didn't grow bigger, but rather condensed, growing smaller and brighter.

Michel's voice came again, this time more stern.

Sebastian stilled. The blue light was now the size of a tennis ball. He cradled it, cupping his hands around it as the light grew brighter, and then he drew it back and pitched it at his father.

I held my breath.

Michel's hands went up, palms flat to meet the ball of blue light. Upon contact, the light exploded, curving around him before dissipating away into nothing. He'd been pushed back a few feet, and that seemed to impress him. He came forward and clapped Sebastian on the shoulder.

Then Michel's gaze lifted to mine.

Instant heat shot to my cheeks. I managed a small, pathetic

wave. Sebastian turned. His black eyebrows drew together, but I couldn't tell if he was frowning or the sun was making him squint.

"Ari. Come down," Michel called.

I hadn't changed or cleaned up since my workout with Bran. *Figures,* I thought. Michel said something to Sebastian and chuckled as the butler walked from beneath the second-story porch where I stood and began to set the patio table for dinner.

Whatever Michel said had Sebastian turning back toward me. His head lifted; his eyes were definitely on me, but I couldn't read them from that distance. Somehow, though, I didn't feel good about it. In fact, goose bumps traveled up my arms and thighs.

And then he was gone.

Sebastian. Gone. Leaving behind a violent whoosh of air that I saw for the barest of seconds, like an eighteen-wheeler hitting mist at seventy miles an hour.

That same air hit me from behind.

I spun around, grabbing the railing for support. "Jesus!"

Sebastian stood there with a crooked grin denting his cheek, his gray eyes lit with amusement. "My dad wants you to stay for dinner."

I released the breath I'd been holding as the shock slowly ebbed from my body. Kind of.

Michel wanted me to stay, but I couldn't help wondering if

his son did too. It was hard to tell with Sebastian. "Ever hear of asking like a normal person?" I asked. "That was crazy."

He gave an innocent shrug and smiled. "Not normal, so . . ."

"Right."

I followed him down the stairs to the patio below.

"You're white as a ghost, Ari," Michel said, pulling out a chair and gesturing for me to sit. "I apologize, as that"—he glanced to the balcony—"was my idea."

I cleared my throat. "I didn't realize you could, uh . . . do that." Whatever *that* was.

"Only the most well-trained or gifted in our family can. But even so, it's a power that requires a period of magical inactivity—rest time, if you will—before it can be used again. Bastian is far behind on his training, but he has talent on his side. Please join us for dinner."

I sat down, grateful because my legs felt weak. After Michel and Sebastian took their seats, platters and drinks were brought out.

"I have the finest chef in the Quarter. I hope you like Cajun food," Michel said as he helped himself to the servings set in the middle of the table. "My chef's cooking was something I thought of often during my imprisonment. Please, help yourself."

Starving, I took a bit of everything and started digging in. Michel talked as we ate, making sure to include me and Sebastian with questions about school and the state of things in the GD.

"So, what was that in the yard, exactly?" I asked during a lull in the conversation. "The ball of light."

"I'm training with my father," Sebastian answered, but the glance between them made me feel as though there was something they weren't saying. "The light ball is basically energy pulled together from everything around us. Energy is there, but most people can't feel it."

"Though some humans can," Michel said between chewing. "Usually if they are sensitive or close to places with strong energy signatures, like ley lines."

"But all witches and warlocks can sense it and use it?"

"Yes. Our unique genes—the thing that separates us from being one hundred percent human—is our ability to recognize and connect with Earth's energy and to utilize it, to have a thought and then make it happen. That is what magic is all about. It has taken thousands of years of evolution, study, and training, and the passing down of knowledge from one generation to the next, in order for us to master the energy and our gifts."

I nodded, stabbing a piece of roasted chicken.

"How was your training with Bran?" Michel sat back and took his wineglass with him. "Better today?"

"It was fine. I actually came by to ask you about the library. When will I be able to see it?"

He regarded me thoughtfully, absently swirling the liquid in his glass. "There is time, you know. Athena will present herself, offer a trade. You for the child, I'm sure."

My grip on my fork went tight. I felt Sebastian stiffen beside me. There was no time. Every minute Violet and my father spent with Athena was a minute too long. How could he expect me to just wait?

"Her indecision," Michel continued, "regarding you . . . I believe she fully intended to kill you herself, which was why she had her second hunter bring you to her prison—revenge on you for killing the first one sent after you. But then when you displayed your power at the Arnaud ball, I suspect Athena began to rethink. She is wondering how best to use you, whether it's better to keep you alive or to kill you. As a god-killer, you'd have many uses."

All of which I knew and Athena had pretty much said. She'd offered me a place with her, a position of power, and all I had to do was submit and become her weapon. Not going to happen, but either she still thought she could manipulate me into service or she planned to finally kill me.

"Sebastian will show you the library in the morning." Michel raised a questioning eyebrow at his son. "Yes?"

Sebastian agreed.

I took a long drink of cold water. "Thank you." My voice was wrapped in relief when I said it. I'd half expected him to go back on his (and the Novem's) promise.

"You don't have any idea where Athena would be keeping my father or Violet?" I asked him.

Michel shook his head. "No. But I suspect she has created another prison near New 2 or she has taken them to her temple. And unfortunately, I don't know where that is. Temples are the gods' best-guarded secrets. Or at least, guarded from us."

"Anything in the library about them?"

"Plenty, I'm sure. Though, to my knowledge, no one has found exact locations. The library is vast, as you'll see, so don't give up hope."

I don't intend to, I thought, shoving another bite into my mouth.

We finished eating, the silence interrupted occasionally by Michel asking a question or commenting on something. I barely paid attention. The sounds beyond the courtyard grew louder as the sun went down. The faint tunes of a saxophone mingled with the hum of pedestrian traffic and the occasional echo of carriage creaks and hooves.

Lights eventually came on in the courtyard, making the tall iron street-style lamps glow yellow. White Christmas lights were wrapped around some of the trees. And the pool was illuminated by underwater interior lights.

"I believe another parade is about to begin. Would you like to watch from the front porch?" Michel placed his napkin on the table and stood.

Sebastian and I followed his lead.

"I should probably go before it gets too crazy," I said.

"Ah. Well, understandable. Sebastian will see you home."

I thanked Michel for dinner, and then he walked toward the house, leaving Sebastian and me standing alone by the table. Awkward and alone.

"One second," he said quickly, and then went after his father. They exchanged words by the stairs before Michel continued up to the second-story balcony and into the house.

"You don't have to see me out," I told him as he came back to the table. "Unless you're going home too."

"No. I have more training to do, but it's fine."

Don't sound so enthused, I thought as I drew in a deep breath, turned, and headed toward the gate.

Seven

Sebastian locked the courtyard gate behind us. "Look, you really don't have to walk me back," I said again.

He took my elbow to direct me through the gathering crowd of tourists and locals, many of whom were decked out in Mardi Gras apparel. "I know, Ari. I want to."

I wasn't practiced with guys. I'd never had a boyfriend, and I didn't know what the hell I was doing, only that I couldn't take this weird tension between us. I wanted answers, facts, honesty, instead of wondering how he felt about me.

I pinched the bridge of my nose and released the pent-up breath I'd been holding, getting jostled from behind by a group trying to pass through the ever-growing crowd. They knocked me closer to Sebastian, so close that I smelled his scent and felt his warmth.

"I don't need an escort," I mumbled, and started off through the crowd.

"Ari."

He was somewhere behind me, blocked by several people. The sounds of energetic brass instruments grew louder and louder. The parade was drawing closer, coming down Royal Street. Colors flashed. Sequins, shiny beads, and glitter dusted over skin, sparkled in the light. Masks of every style and color bobbed in the crowd.

Laughter, voices, and music blended together.

I was hit hard from the side and lost my balance. Shit. Hands wrapped around my arm and elbow as Sebastian's voice called from somewhere in the crowd.

"Thanks," I breathed, turning toward the Good Samaritan who'd saved me from being trampled by a bunch of inebriated revelers.

A huge form in a black cloak stood there, regarding me through the eyeholes of a smooth gold Mardi Gras mask. People bumped into him, but he was like an island that did not budge. His head dipped in acknowledgment, and then he melded into the crowd, and I stood there wondering if I'd just come into contact with one of Michel's mysterious guards.

The press of people closed around me again, but Sebastian made it to my side and together we weaved our way toward the sidewalk. The crowd moved back with us in a uniform wave as the first float of the parade turned the corner. Great. We were about to be sardines.

I didn't like crowds, didn't like being pushed and squished and trapped. It made me angry and just a little bit panicky.

I tripped on the sidewalk curb. Sebastian's arm slipped around my waist and kept me from falling into the people in front of me. They shifted, and we became plastered against the wall of a storefront.

Well, *I* was plastered against the storefront. Sebastian was plastered against my back. The entire front of his body was molded against me.

Sebastian's arms tightened around my waist. His head dipped until his mouth was close enough to my ear so I could hear him above the crowd. "Goddamn parades. Hold on. I'm getting us out of here." And when he spoke, it seemed to drown out everything around me. "Don't be afraid."

And then we were gone.

Weightless.

The ground at my feet suddenly disappeared along with everything else.

A scream lodged in my throat, coming out broken and pathetic.

And then we were sitting on a wide ledge. High above Jackson Square. Christ, he'd blinked me to—I gazed above me.

Not just any ledge. *Oh God, oh God, oh God.*

"It helps if you breathe."

"I think I might kill you," I said in a near whisper.

Sebastian's shoulder bumped mine as he tried to hide his smile. "Well, you've got time, because we'll be up here for an hour or so before I have enough power again to get us down. I didn't think you'd be afraid of heights."

I glared at him. "I'm not afraid of heights. I am, apparently, afraid of disappearing from solid ground and then reappearing on a ledge."

I rubbed a hand down my face and then blew out a loud exhale, trying to calm my drumming pulse and letting my gaze settle over Jackson Square below.

We sat on top of St. Louis Cathedral, on the ledge that went around the base of the tall middle steeple. Sebastian sat beside me, his legs swinging, leaning back against the steeple wall as though this was a usual perch.

The breeze was chilly. Lights from the boats on the river gleamed and bobbed, and the square was filled with people. The brassy music from the parade wafted through the streets and mingled with the conversations below.

Once I got over the shock, being up there was pretty damn cool—looking down on the world, the activity, the music, and yet separated from it in our own little world.

"I knew you'd like this," Sebastian said with quiet satisfaction.

His head stayed back against the wall, but he turned it to meet my gaze. Humor swam in those gray eyes, but everything else about him was still. "You're reading my emotions?"

He shrugged and didn't answer.

"I take it you've come here before."

"More than once," he said, staring out over the square.

"Why did you kiss me that day?" The question was out of my mouth before I could stop it. Heat crept up my neck and into my face, but I didn't look away from him because, as embarrassed as I was, I wanted to know the answer.

His lips dipped into a wry smile, driving a deep crease into his cheek. One raven eyebrow lifted a bit higher than the other. The storm clouds in his eyes seemed to give way to a lighter shade of gray. "Why did you kiss me back?"

Time suspended—a long, unforgiving, humiliating space that was filled by me looking like the world's greatest dumbass as my mind floundered for something to say.

Sebastian drew up one leg and turned more toward me, his shoulder pressing against the wall.

What would he say? That he'd kissed me because I was there, lying on top of him at Gabonna's, our faces so close, so why not? My stomach knotted. *Please don't let it be something like that.*

"I kissed you," he began, his voice calm, blunt, and honest, "because you caught me off guard. Because that day, even if it was only just a few hours we spent together, I felt normal and understood with you. There are things I can sense and feel from people. That's why I didn't want to help you at first; the similarities I felt between us . . . I just balked, I guess. Didn't want to get involved." He smiled. "That didn't last very long, did it?"

"No," I replied, returning the smile.

"And then when I woke up in Gabonna's, the way you were looking at me . . ." His Adam's apple slid up and down. He looked away then and a faint blush appeared on his pale skin. Then he looked back. "I got caught up, wasn't really thinking, just . . . feeling." He paused, giving me an intense look. "But I don't regret it. Do you?"

I shook my head. "But . . . in the cemetery. You ran when you saw the vision of me as a gorgon." I wanted to rub the sour, burning feeling creeping into my chest. "I know you came back and fought, but"—I drew in a deep breath and released it—"I'm not sure how you feel now, or what, if anything, there is between you and me."

I couldn't look at him anymore, so I focused on his hand resting on his knee and the silver piece inlaid in the leather band around his wrist.

"Seeing you like that scared the shit out of me, Ari, more because Athena had you and I knew I couldn't fight her alone. I had to get Dub and Crank away and go for my father, so I ran. But I won't lie to you. Seeing your curse, the vision of it, it did scare me."

I bit the inside of my cheek. It hurt to hear that. But it was honest, and how could I blame him when I felt the same? "It scared me, too." My eyes stung. "I hate it." I stared out over the square below. "I don't want to become that . . . thing."

He reached over and slid his hand into mine. It was warm and slightly roughened on the palms.

We stayed that way for a long time, just watching the night pass by on our perch above the Quarter. And even though there were no words about an "us," there didn't need to be. His hand in mine was answer enough.

"My father is wrong about waiting," Sebastian said.

I didn't need to ask him what he meant. More than anything, I knew that if we waited for Athena to show herself, to reveal her plan, Violet and my father might never recover from their time spent with the goddess.

"We need to strike first," I said. "Find a way into her realm and take back what is ours."

His hand tightened on mine. "She won't be expecting that."

And surprise might be the *only* thing going for us.

Eight

The sun was up fully by the time I stepped off the streetcar and headed down Royal Street for another day at Presby. Morning light bathed the French Quarter, turning it into a sparkling jewel.

Motor vehicles were prohibited in the Quarter, which took the place back a hundred years and increased the number of mules and carriages. The tourists loved it. I did too—no constant drone of engines, no horns or brakes, no smell of exhaust to clog the air. Only trash and delivery trucks were allowed through, and those just came at off-peak hours.

I could've taken one of the many carriages that waited near Canal Street to carry people into the Quarter, but I chose to walk the several blocks to Jackson Square. I gazed up at the tall arched second-story windows as I passed the old Cabildo building next to St. Louis Cathedral. As crazy as it sounded, some of the very first settlers of New Orleans back in the 1700s and 1800s were currently sitting in those offices and running the city.

Sebastian was waiting for me outside of Presby. The fact that students passed by him in uniform and he was standing there in torn jeans and a faded old concert T-shirt made me smile. The rebel in me could *totally* relate.

I stopped in front of him. "They're not going to let you stay in school dressed like that. I got a huge lecture for wearing a black shirt the other day."

He glanced at my outfit, which didn't really diverge from my normal fashion, and arched an eyebrow. Black cargo pants, white tank, gray zip-up hoodie, with a τέρας blade strapped to my thigh and a dagger in my boot.

"What? Pants are black. Shirt is white. The blade stays." I grinned wider. "Because I'm special."

He laughed, a deep, scruffy sound that warmed me to my toes. "I think our dear Presby principal would miss me if I wasn't in his office at least once a week," he said. "He expects me, and I'd hate to upset him. Always thinking of others, I am. . . ."

My laughter felt good and a little foreign. "Right. Your dad told me you only have a few more classes before you graduate. You going to stay on after that?"

"Someone has to keep you in line," he said. "My dad says you're a good influence on me. I'm back in high school, going to attend Presby's college. . . . You might just be his *favorite* person at the moment."

"Always thinking of others, I am." I repeated his remark with a laugh. "So, we're cool with going into the library?"

"Yeah. My dad already let the teachers know you won't be in class."

Sebastian had left the GD early to talk to Michel before classes began, just to make sure I'd have access to the library and not have to deal with any red tape the other Novem heads might have thrown my way.

He shook his head and held out his hand. I took it like it was the most natural thing on earth, and it felt that way too. "Why the funny look?" I asked.

He pulled me toward the school. "I'm pretty sure you're the only student who ever attended Presby armed."

I laughed. "Please. Everyone here is armed. Just not with blades."

The bell rang as we entered. Students hurried to classes, leaving us walking down a very quiet, echoing hallway. We passed classroom after classroom, the lone student or two, snippets of

lectures from open doors, the hum of recitals and music lesson
and then we went up a set of wide steps.

"Ari," Sebastian said, stopping as we hit the turn in the stair
"I know I can't go into the library with you, but whatever yo
learn in there . . . I can help on the outside. Athena screwed u
my life too."

"I know she did," I responded quietly.

"And I know you're the type who likes to do things alone
he said, arching his brow. "It takes one to know one. But"—h
grabbed my arm and pulled me into the corner as a group o
students went by—"don't run off and do this by yourself."

Over his shoulder I spotted a few of the students throwin
glances back at me as they went down the steps. I waited fo
them to disappear before I said, "She only wants me, Sebastiar
There's no point in anyone else getting hurt."

He actually rolled his eyes. "That's great. And you're missin
the entire point."

"No, I'm not."

"Hell yes, you are." He grabbed me by the shoulders. W
were deep in the corner now. Sebastian's body blocked most c
me from view should anyone walk by. He smelled clean—tin
notes of shampoo, deodorant, and laundry detergent. "If yo
think I'm just going to say good luck and wave good-bye as yo
go off facing Athena, you're dumber than I thought."

"Gee, thanks." This was stupid. I understood what he was saying. That we were in this together. He had a stake because of what Athena had done to his father, and because he cared about Violet. He wanted in, and he sure as hell didn't like the fact that I was the only one who had access to the library.

"You're just going to have to trust me," I said. I didn't want him to get hurt, to be yet another person Athena sank her claws into.

And the bad part about it was that he knew exactly what was going through my mind. I pushed against him, but he didn't budge, just gazed down at me, his jaw tight, red lips drawn into a firm line, and eyes smoldering.

I shoved harder, squeezing between him and the wall, and ran up the rest of the stairs, my boots pounding in time with my heart.

I went a few feet down the hall before I realized I had no clue where to go, which was totally embarrassing since I had to turn in the middle of the hallway and wait for him.

Sebastian came up the stairs and moved down the hall toward me with laserlike intent. Everything about him seemed calm, dark, and intense. I swallowed, feeling pretty stupid for even attempting my Go It Alone mantra on him . . . and myself.

He only stopped when he was toe to toe with me.

"You're not doing this without me." His words were tight

and his eyes like glinting steel. "I haven't been training my ass off with my father for nothing. You need me. You might not want me, but you need me."

With that, he marched around me and toward a flight of stairs that led to the third floor.

All I knew was that he could turn me into a confused, breathless idiot one second and piss me off the next. *Might as well add that ability to his list of powers,* I thought darkly, following him up the steps.

Sebastian was the second most powerful member of the Lamarliere family. Not only a rare warlock like his father but a vampire like his mother. And she was a Bloodborn, born of both a vampire mother and father, the strongest kind of vampire there was. Sebastian had the potential, or at least the genes, to be extremely powerful. Having him on my side was a bonus and a gift I shouldn't ignore.

And whether he believed it or not, I didn't *want* to do this alone. I just didn't want anyone else to get hurt. He was right, but that didn't make it any easier to accept. I'd spent most of my life facing things alone. Being in New 2 had changed that. Now I had Sebastian and Michel. I had Henri, Crank, Dub, and Violet. But that also meant more hurt and pain if something happened to them because of this thing with Athena. And I wasn't sure I could deal with that.

In the end, though, I needed help. Sebastian was one of only a handful of people in New 2 who I trusted. And as a Novem heir, he had access to things many others did not.

"The third floor is mainly for administration," Sebastian told me as we came to a desk. A woman looked up. "Back again, Bastian?" she asked, eyeing his street clothes. "Your father said you were coming. Go on back."

"Does she know about the library?" I whispered as we walked down a long corridor with offices on both sides.

"No. No one knows except the Novem heads and their next in lines. She thinks I'm using the private study. You'll see." We turned a corner and walked toward a huge set of double doors at the end of the hallway.

Sebastian slipped a card into a security scanner attached to the wall by the door. A lock slid back. "This leads to the study. No one comes back here without a card, and there are only nine cards. This one is my father's."

Sebastian opened one side of the double door and stepped back to let me enter. I expected a room or at least another hallway, but it was an area the size of a walk-in closet and another tall door in front of me.

"It's iron, blood-spelled and warded nine times. The wards are changed once a week. You have to know the combination to unravel all nine wards to get it to open and you have to be blood-related. And then there's security inside the library itself."

"And you know the combination?"

"My dad taught me this morning."

Sebastian pulled a safety pin from his pocket and pricked his finger, then placed his hand on the intricately carved door. It contained thousands of small symbols and lines, swirls and patterns. A soft blue light appeared beneath his finger and he began to trace one of the patterns.

He traced nine patterns. Each one stayed blue and glowing until he finished. It was a maze that I never could've repeated if I'd tried. Then the outline of the door began to glow until the blue turned to white and the door popped open with an audible sigh. Sebastian turned to me. "The real secret is inside."

He pushed open the heavy door. It groaned, sending a shiver up my spine as I stepped inside a large study. It was everything you'd think a wealthy library should look like—dark paneling, huge stone fireplace, Persian rug, leather furniture, study tables and desks, and shelves of books that ringed the room, so tall there was a ladder on a track that could be pushed around to get whatever book you wanted.

"So where do we star—" I frowned. "Wait a minute. I thought you weren't allowed inside. This isn't it, is it?"

He rocked back on his heels and smiled. "Nope."

He guided me across the large room to the corner and

stopped. Bookshelves. A plant. An enormous old vase. I wasn't sure what he was looking at . . . maybe something on the shelf?

I stepped closer.

Sebastian stared at the six-and-a-half-foot-tall vase. It was so big I could've crawled inside it and curled up easily. It had two sloping handles on each side with specks of black paint. The opening at the top was wider than my shoulders. It had a slim neck, and a body that fattened out in the middle and then slimmed down again before widening out at the base.

It looked incredibly ancient, made of clay or terra-cotta, I guessed. There were lines and symbols and figures stamped around its body.

The thing that stood out the most was the long, jagged crack down the front, from the neck of the vase to just above the base. It was deep and dark in the center, showing just how thick the vase was.

"Okay," I said, obviously missing something. "What are we looking at?"

"Anesidora's Jar. Otherwise known as Pandora's Box."

I blinked, looking at him skeptically. "What?" A nervous laugh escaped me. He wasn't laughing back—not a good sign. I glanced from him to the jar. His expression stayed serious. "Uh, hate to break it to you, but this isn't a box."

"It never was. It was always a jar. Some dude translated the original Greek word into Latin and called it a box instead of a jar. And the term just kind of stayed."

"I don't understand what this has to do with the library."

"This *is* the library, Ari. Inside this jar is—Well, here, let me show you."

He reached for my hand, but I stepped back. He was playing some sort of joke. He had to be. Right? A current of wariness swept through me.

"Look, I know it's crazy, but . . . this jar was given to some of the earliest *doué*. A gift from a god no one can name. It's a place for all things important, sacred to the ancestors of the Novem families and passed down as a library for our secrets, a place where no god can go. It holds artifacts, tablets, books, scrolls. Our entire history is in this jar. It can't be destroyed and it holds anything you put inside it."

Yeah, right. "I thought you weren't supposed to open Pandora's Box."

He shrugged. "Wouldn't know about that. Probably just a myth."

I lifted an eyebrow. "Really. Just a *myth*," I said in a flat tone, and waved a hand at him. "Says the warlock vampire to the gorgon."

A slow grin drew his lips apart. "I see your point."

I smiled despite myself, and then shook my head, turning

back around to face the enormous jar. "So, what, press a secret combination and it opens? Or do I just pull off the lid?" The thing was big enough to hold a bunch of books and scrolls, so all I had to do was open it and hope to hell they were in a language I could understand.

"No, you just pull open the crack and step inside." At my blink, he explained: "Pandora never opened her 'box.' It cracked. You can read about it inside if you want. It's all there. Way more than you'd ever want to know. . . ."

"You're not coming?"

He shook his head. "Can't. I'm not supposed to have access to the library until I take over from my father. It's the same for all the heirs."

"But didn't your dad sneak you in?"

"When I was little, yeah, but he was breaking Novem rules when he did, so don't go around repeating that."

"So how will I know what to look for, how to find the stuff on Athena? I don't suppose the Novem uses the Dewey decimal system."

"Funny. No, the Keeper will help you. He'll explain the rules. Make sure you follow them."

"Just so you know—I mean, I know this is New 2, the place for all things bizarre and everything, but this . . . this is way out there."

He gave a soft laugh. "When my dad brought me here, this thing scared me to death."

"Is that your way of saying boy Sebastian was braver than me?"

"You'll be fine. There's no danger inside as long as you follow the rules. You can leave whenever you want."

I drew in a deep breath and stepped up to the jar, trying to shake off the creep factor. It was just so . . . strange, the idea that I was supposed to go *inside* the jar. I squared my shoulders. I could do this. How hard could it be? Sebastian had gone with his dad when he was little, and nothing as little as a crack in a vase was going to stop me from finding Violet or my father.

I reached out, braced my thumbs on the outside of the jar, and slipped my fingers into the cold, jagged crack.

NINE

AND ONCE AGAIN ARI FALLS DOWN THE RABBIT HOLE, I thought as the edges of the clay jar peeled back, splintering with a blinding light that crept up my fingers, hands, and arms like electrified sparks.

The hard edges of the jar buckled, collapsing back. My heart pounded hard as I ducked inside, into the bright light ringed with blackness.

I released the crack as I went, stepping fully into the jar and then straightening. The energy humming through me was already fading with the light. White dots danced in my vision. I didn't move, didn't take a single step forward.

Music came like a leaf riding a gentle breeze. Italian opera mingled with the telltale skip and scratch of a record spinning, the music distant and echoing and brassy like it came from a horn. The white dots in my vision began to fade, and a vast room washed in orange candlelight came into focus, its walls and edges hidden in darkness. There were no boundaries; there was no way to mark the size of the room. It was like an island library in the blackness of space.

Several feet in front of me stretched a marble counter, and behind it was a large area with long tables, chairs, and lamps for study. Beyond that were row upon row of tall shelves and narrow aisles that went so far back, they disappeared into the darkness. The scope was beyond what I could've imagined, and I knew there was no way in hell I could ever go through this place without help.

I swallowed, reminding myself of my purpose, and stepped toward the counter. I glanced over my shoulder to see the massive crack dimly lit in the blackness. Either I had shrunk, or the crack had grown to twice the size it was on the outside of the jar. A tremor—the kind that comes when you suddenly realize how small and insignificant you are, how quickly you might become lost—ran through me. This wasn't just the inside of the jar—this was another dimension.

I approached the marble counter, each end so long that they, too, disappeared into the black space surrounding the library. The top of the counter came to just below my chest. It was smooth and white, and I knew it would be cold to the touch, though I kept my hands down at my sides.

"Study topic?"

I jumped at the words, spinning around at the strange male voice. Jesus! I grabbed my chest, making sure my heart was still there and beating because it sure as hell felt like it had just been scared right out of me.

A figure stood behind the counter to my right. And it wasn't human.

I wasn't sure what I'd expected, but it wasn't this . . . thing. "What are you?" I blurted out.

Bronze eyelids blinked over eyes made of white stone inset with round brown disks for irises. "Automaton. The Keeper. Study topic, please."

Its outer "skin" was made of tiny plates of bronze that allowed movement. It wore a Greek-style toga, which was odd, seeing as it was made of metal—unless it was anatomically correct, and then the clothing definitely made sense. It must've been filled with gears and a power source, and obviously had a mechanism that allowed speech. Whoever had built this was a genius or a magician. Maybe both.

"Study topic, please."

I cleared my throat. "Um, right, okay . . . ," I said, trying to get back on track. "I'd like anything you have on Athena, her temple, her weapons, her weaknesses. Anything about the war between Athena and the other gods. Oh, and curses, ones made by the gods, and any stories or myths about people overcoming them would be good."

The Keeper turned, walked down the counter a few steps, and opened a gate I hadn't noticed. He stood back and I entered the study area. The Keeper didn't frighten me so much as surprise me, and I didn't feel threatened—if I had, I'd have been halfway to the crack by now.

At the edge of the study area I found the source of the music—an old record player box with a huge horn on the top. The song reached its climax, becoming louder and more dramatic, cresting and cresting, then crashing in waves of beautiful notes and intense emotion that surprised me.

"What's that song?" My curiosity came out before I could stop it.

"'Nessun Dorma.' In your tongue, 'None Shall Sleep.' It is an aria from the final act of *Turandot*, an opera composed by Giacomo Puccini," he answered in a monotone voice. A talking encyclopedia. "It is sung by Calaf, the unknown prince, to the cold Princess Turandot. She recoils at the thought of marrying him. He tells her if she guesses his name by dawn, she may execute him and be free. If she fails, she must marry him. The princess decrees that none of her subjects shall sleep that night until they discover his name. Should they fail her, they all will die."

"That's horrible," I muttered. She sounded as brutal and unfair as Athena. "What happens in the end?" The record had ended and was playing a chorus of static, skip, and scratch over and over again.

"Dawn arrives. The princess and her subjects have failed to discover the prince's name. He tells her his name, allowing her to make the choice to execute him or love him. She chooses to love him." The Keeper pulled out a chair. "Please take a seat. I will return."

I stood near the corner of a table and watched the tall bronze automaton go to the old record player, lift the needle, and set it at the beginning of the opera again. Then it disappeared down one of the long aisles.

I didn't sit, but instead browsed some of the rows near the study area. The shelves were packed with books, manuscripts, scrolls, and tablets. Other shelves held artifacts: boxes, jars, small statues, shields, weapons. I moved slowly, scanning, taking it all in.

The light grew dimmer as I went, but there was enough for me to see that there were things from nearly every era of civilization—that I knew of, anyway—and some that didn't seem to have a time period at all. The aisle ended in an area with tables and items too big for the shelves: tall statues of people, gods, and animals; an actual chariot; a massive oil painting; a throne made of gold. There were chests and plates on the table full of gold, bronze, and silver coins.

Nearest to me was a long table made of thick black wood. A small marble basket containing a marble infant didn't seem to fit with the other things I'd seen so far, but maybe that was due to the two marble hands clenching the sides of the basket from behind, broken at the wrists.

"The material you requested is up front."

"Jeez!" That thing was going to give me a heart attack. For a metal robot, the Keeper was eerily quiet as it moved. Or maybe I'd just been too lost in thought.

"What's with this statue?" I asked it.

"Those are the hands of Zeus. And that is the child fated to kill him."

The Keeper turned. With a parting look at the strange broken sculpture, I trailed behind the bronze automaton back down the aisle as he spouted off the library rules, which basically went something like:

Don't rub the books, tablets, or scrolls.

Don't blow on them.

Don't alter them.

Don't take notes.

Don't read aloud from them.

And, above all, don't carry them past the counter.

We stopped at one of the front tables, where four tall stacks of books, a pile of scrolls, and two clay tablets sat. Oh boy.

The Keeper went to the counter, reached beneath it, and retrieved a long, rectangular glass panel. It curved downward at each end, so when he placed it on the table, it was raised off the surface by five inches or so. Around the panel were etchings in glass, thousands of minuscule symbols.

"This will allow you to understand what you see. Set it carefully over your text and you will be able to read in the glass what is written there. Remember, do not take notes or bring anything beyond the counter."

He began to walk away.

"What happens if I do?"

He stopped and turned around, his fake eyes giving me the willies. "You forfeit your life. It is that simple."

I watched him go down one of the aisles, feeling like the temperature in the room had dropped by ten degrees. No emotion. No care either way. The Keeper's reply drove home the rules more than anyone else could have. He'd be completely indifferent to my death. There would be no hesitation or remorse.

Not dwelling, I pulled out a chair and started with a stone tablet. It was small, the size of a paperback book, and was filled

with tiny linear slashes and symbols pressed into
placed it carefully beneath the glass. Words began to
within the glass—a strange sort of magic I didn't qu

I read about a Sumerian woman named Tiash
witch who removed a curse placed on her by the go

Interesting story, but it didn't offer any clues
witch removed the curse other than "untangling"
inside of my cheek, wondering if it was really that s
needed to do to rid myself of Athena's curse was to
who could untangle the words Athena had spoken
those years ago.

When my mind grew tired and refused to hold a
mation, I took the glass panel back to the count
held the gate open, and I walked to the crack in
pulled it apart, and stepped into the Novem's stu

And came face-to-face with Josephine Arna
Arnaud family. A Bloodborn vampire and Sebas

Josephine oozed wealth and old-world soph
a single hair out of place or wrinkle in her expen
dark eyes burned with intellect. She was a few h
but she looked like a beautiful young woman.

She was also a complete and total bitch, ri
Athena.

We eyed each other for a second, and then I stepped around ıer, walking through the cloud of her elegant perfume. I didn't ave anything to say. She gave my father up to Athena and anted to use me to increase her own power. She didn't give a ıit about me at all. And the feeling was mutual.

I was halfway to the door before she spoke in her cultured rench accent. "Find what you were looking for?"

I hesitated, knowing I should keep going, but I walked back stand in front of her. "If I did, I wouldn't tell you, Josephine. ›u never could help me, could you?" I asked, remembering her fer to remove the curse in exchange for my allegiance.

"No one can remove your curse. It's too old, too powerful, › tangled, and spoken by a god." She laughed and shook her ad. "Your naïveté is astounding. In three and a half years, you l become a full-blown gorgon." She cocked her chin. "And my ndson will have learned a great life lesson."

Like she cared about Sebastian's personal growth. All she ed about was power.

"His interest in you is merely rebellion. You are differ- Forbidden. Something he *knows* is wrong." Her dark eyes eled over my features. "He sees beauty now, is lured by it, ı though he knows what lies beneath is evil. So intriguing, flirting with danger." She flicked a glance at the jar. "Pandora the same way, you know? A deceptive package. The Greek

writers called her *Kalon Kakon*, a beautiful evil. It won't be long before you destroy those around you, just like she did."

My fists clenched hard. "And if that happens, Josephine, if I turn into a monster, I'll be coming for you first, and there isn't a damn thing you can do to stop me."

TEN

I TURNED MY BACK AND WALKED AWAY FROM JOSEPHINE, KNOWING that right then she could've snapped my neck, killed me before I even made it to the iron door. She could've, but she wouldn't have.

The Novem had agreed to keep me in the city, shield me from Athena, and allow me into their library. And I knew the only reason Josephine had agreed was because she thought me going after Athena was a suicide mission.

Whatever. I'd spent my life proving people wrong. What was one more?

I shoved the tall iron door open, went four steps, and then pushed the double doors wide. There'd always be a target on my back when it came to Josephine. The only question was when she'd choose to strike.

Every step I took down the stairs, I let out a little more of the anger I'd been holding in. By the time I got to the first floor, I was less angry but way more irritated, cussing under my breath and saying all the rude, obnoxious things I'd wanted to say to Josephine. I ignored the looks thrown my way as I marched into the large study hall, her comments about Sebastian echoing in my head.

I knew Josephine's game. Her clever words had been designed to sink into my psyche in my quiet moments, when I was alone and not feeling confident, when her words would cut me the most. I saw it for what it was, but the worst part was that she might be right. If I didn't find a way to reverse the curse, things might go exactly like she said. I'd be a gorgon and Sebastian would walk away from me.

I found a quiet table, slapped my backpack down, and jerked out my notebook, throwing a glare over my shoulder at the group of kids sitting at the nearest table. They turned away quickly.

Like I was some kind of freak show.

Whatever. Get to work and forget them. They don't matter.

I sat down, drew in long breath to steady myself, and started writing down everything I could remember about what I'd read in the library. After a few notes, I was able to sink into my task and forget Josephine and the fact that the entire school seemed bent on ogling me at every opportunity.

The sudden squeak of the chair across from me made me look up, my pen skipping over the edge of the paper. A guy dropped into the chair.

"Well, if it isn't the Moon Queen herself."

Images of the Arnaud ball slammed into me before I could stop them. Spinning around and around on the dance floor amid a sea of beautiful gowns and masks. Like a glittering dream . . .

Gabriel Baptiste, Novem heir and Bloodborn vampire, rocked back in the chair, crossed his arms over his chest, and stared at me, his lips twisting into a playful smile.

My cheeks flared hot. I'd danced in Gabriel's arms during the ball. I'd flirted with him and nearly allowed him, a masked stranger, to kiss my neck—and possibly do more had Sebastian not showed up.

First Josephine and now Gabriel. I shook my head at my shitty luck.

"My father told me you'd be attending Presby. Didn't quite believe him. But"—he smiled—"here you are."

I rolled my eyes.

"Everyone is talking about you. Word spreads fast, you know. Gorgon. God-killer. Freak. You're to be our savior, our protector from Athena, is that it?"

His mocking words held an edge to them, as though his

male Bloodborn ego couldn't handle the idea of me saving the Novem or, more to the point, him. Sebastian had been right. Bloodborns had enormous egos.

Two other guys dropped down beside him, and a girl stood behind his chair, hugging textbooks to her chest. I sat back slowly, setting my pen down and closing my notebook. I regarded them with the slightly bored, uncaring look that I'd perfected years ago.

I almost smiled. If they thought they could intimidate me . . . Amateurs. *Try facing a psychotic goddess of war.*

"Rumor is you're going after Athena," the girl said. "Rumor is they let you into the library."

Something no one was supposed to know. "And you are?"

"Anne Hawthorne. My mother is head of the Hawthorne family. I'm to follow in her footsteps."

A witch, then. The Hawthornes, Cromleys, and Lamarlieres were the three witch families in the Novem. Anne's mother, Rowen, was in the Council of Nine meeting when it was decided that I'd attend the school and would be granted access to the library. I didn't know why the hell they called it a secret library if everyone seemed to know about it.

"We're all Novem heirs," Gabriel said. "So we know things the rest of our families don't. We'll be running things soon."

The way he said it . . . like a threat, like I was a problem they'd be dealing with one day. Gabriel Asshole Baptiste was playing his own version of Novem head already.

I shoved my notebook into my backpack. "Look, Gabriel, if you have a point to all this, then get to it."

He eyed me for a drawn-out moment. "The way to Athena isn't in any book."

I gave him a "So what?" look.

"Come on, Gabriel, let's go," Anne said, glancing around and suddenly going pale. Sebastian had entered the hall.

Gabriel ignored her. "I know where you should look."

"Where?"

"The ruins."

"I thought the ruins are supposed to be off-limits," I said, noticing that Sebastian had spotted us, and his mood was black. The tension in the room spiked.

Gabriel regarded Sebastian as he moved toward us, and then he turned back to me, humor playing on his lips. I couldn't believe I had ever let this guy get close to me. "The Novem makes the rules. We break them. Isn't that how it works? My friends and I go there to . . . play." To hunt. His meaning was obvious, and he meant it to be. "We see her disgusting creatures there sometimes. You might want to have a look, try to capture one of them. Just a thought."

"Why are you telling me this?" Because it wasn't out of

the goodness of his heart; I was pretty sure Gabriel would just love to see me go into the ruins of Midtown and never come back.

"If we scratch your back, maybe one day you'll scratch ours." He paused. "You should come to our Mardi Gras party on Friday." He let his chair fall forward and stood up.

Sebastian blocked his path. I rose slowly as the air between them crackled.

Finally Sebastian stepped around Gabriel and headed for me.

As Gabriel walked away with his cronies, Anne tossed a look over her shoulder, her interest in Sebastian pretty damn clear. The bell rang and students began shoving books into bags and filing out the door.

Sebastian dropped his backpack on the table. "What the hell did he want?"

"He said I should look in the ruins to find Athena."

"Sounds like something he'd say." Sebastian was quiet for a long moment. "You want to get out of here and go to Gabonna's for lunch?"

"Love to."

I gathered my stuff and left Presby, still fuming over Gabriel. He was no different from Josephine and some of the other Novem heads I'd met. I'd faced all nine of them and come away with the realization that most of them lived and breathed intrigue, power, and politics. Even Michel played the game to some degree. I guess you had to if you wanted to hold your own against types like Josephine.

Power and politics were the reasons Josephine had "helped" my mother and had tried to use me. My curse was a tool to her. To Athena. To a lot of people in the Novem. I might've been flattered if only the reason had been different.

Sebastian and I walked to Gabonna's, the restaurant and jazz club on St. Ann Street. It was the same place he'd taken me when I got the migraine from hell after visiting the voodoo priest Jean Solomon.

The same place where I'd woken up in his arms. Where he'd kissed me.

The door was held open by a three-foot-tall statute of an alligator playing the saxophone. I followed Sebastian inside and slid into a corner booth. After ordering sandwiches and drinks, he said, "Don't listen to Gabriel."

The piano player walked by, gave a nod of greeting to Sebastian, and then sat down on his bench. A slow, easy melody filled the restaurant.

"I don't plan to," I answered. "But I was thinking as we were walking here. He might be onto something." I reached into my backpack and pulled out my notebook. "I found out the gods create their own realms to house their temples and palaces. Like a different dimension. It's an automatic security system. Other gods can't pass into the realm unless the god who made the realm allows them in. But humans can pass through, though I couldn't find out why that is. I read stories where people in the past accidentally passed through a doorway into a different realm, or went in search of the land of the gods and found it."

Pam, our waitress, arrived and set our drinks on the table.

"Sebastian," I said, leaning closer to him and feeling like we might actually have a chance at finding Violet and my father. "All we have to do is find the doorway. I bet it's in the ruins. It'd be the best place to hide it. Easy access for her hunters and creatures to come and go, right?"

Sebastian thought for a little while. "Good way for her to have kept tabs all these years. The ruins would be the perfect cover."

The question was, why did Athena have so much interest in New 2? Could it be just because of me, my mother, and my father? Or was there more to it than that?

"I also found out that Athena was able to kill most of the gods in her own pantheon, the Olympians, because they trusted her, they were family. And it was easy for her to kill them because once she'd offed Zeus and had his shield, the Aegis, it protected her from the other gods. It made her indestructible. Apparently, after the war there were only a few gods left from random families. . . ."

"No reason why, though? Why she started her killing spree to begin with?"

I shook my head. "No, nothing. Maybe she just lost it, you know? After thousands of years, she could've cracked."

Our sandwiches came and we ate in thoughtful silence. The more I considered it, the more I believed the doorway was somewhere in the ruins.

"We should become the hunters," I said.

"What? Like hunt down one of her minions?"

I washed my bite down with a drink. "Yeah, and make it tell us how it gets here, where Athena keeps her prisoners."

"Remind me not to get on your bad side. You're not serious, are you?"

Was I? Could I torture information out of another living thing? I groaned, slid my hands over the tabletop, and let my head fall on my hands. "I don't know," I muttered on the way down. I didn't want to be like that, but at the same time, when I thought of what Violet and my father were going through, I just might do anything.

Sebastian's hand touched my back. I lifted my head as his arm slid around my shoulders and he pulled me closer. "Just listen to the music. Take your mind off things for a minute. It's okay to do that, you know?"

"I know." I let my head rest against him as the music continued.

⟡ ⟡ ⟡

We stayed at Gabonna's for nearly an hour before going back to Presby to finish out the day. Bran gave me another brutal workout, but this time I was faster on the "power draw" and he actually paid me a compliment—miracle of miracles. I knew he was right; the more I used my power, the more comfortable it'd become. Though I was still far from feeling *comfort*. Bran was so pleased that he told me to come to the Ramsey Black and Gold Masque, his family's annual Mardi Gras party. He wasn't surprised when I passed on the invitation. The thought of being in a crowd, having to talk and smile and act polite, sounded more exhausting than it was worth.

Sebastian and I took it easy and people-watched in the square after school and then ate dinner at one of the cafés nearby. Once darkness settled over the city, we decided to stroll up the Riverwalk before heading over to catch the streetcar for home.

The Riverwalk at night was the place to be. Streetlamps burned, couples strolled, gamblers went in and out of the newly restored Harrah's. Laughter and conversation mixed with the sound of the street performers playing their trumpets and saxophones. Vendors lined the walk, which paralleled the river, selling flowers, jewelry, masks, and beads. I took a deep inhale of the cold air saturated with Mississippi River and the salty tang of the Gulf of Mexico beyond.

"You sure you don't want to go to the party?" Sebastian asked, bumping me with his shoulder.

"Yeah, I'm sure. I'd rather go back to the GD and crash."

"Me too, but you still have to check it out. The Black and Gold is a pretty cool sight, see?" He nodded ahead of us.

The *Creole Queen* was docked in the water alongside the walk. And the paddleboat wasn't something you could miss; her railings were strung with lights that reflected off the water and made the *Queen* look as though she floated on sequins.

She was packed, too, with Mardi Gras revelers all dressed in black and gold.

Several costumed guests had gathered in groups on the Riverwalk in front of the boat, talking, laughing, and clinking their champagne glasses together as lively jazz wafted from the back of the boat. Tourists snapped pictures and watched the party; the black and gold costumes drew a lot of spectators.

Eyes peered through the oval holes of gorgeous masks, making me think of Violet and how much she'd love to see this. The plain gold ones worn by the men—unadorned, smooth, and covering the forehead to the tip of the nose—gave me the creeps more than any of the others. When they looked at me . . . it was like being stared at by an old-world predator. They turned their heads like silent puppets, seeming suspended for a moment in time, their eyes glittering, black and mysterious.

Despite the eerie masks, the sight was beautiful, like being in an elegant dream of sparkling lights and aristocratic make-believe.

We found a bench in a dark spot away from the crowd. I angled my body so that I could stare at the boat, completely taken with the image. "You can go. To the party. You don't have to stay on my account," I said over my shoulder. "Michel's probably there, right?"

"Probably." He draped his arm over the back of the bench, and I found myself leaning against him. His head dipped and his breath fanned the side of my neck when he spoke. "I'm good. Right where I want to be."

I was glad he couldn't see my idiotic grin.

Eleven

I sat once again at the study table in the Novem's bizarre secret library. The old record player belted out another rousing song. "What are we listening to this time?" I asked the Keeper as he deposited another stack of materials for me to read.

"Vivaldi. *The Four Seasons.* The one playing now is the winter concerto. Are you finished with these?"

"Yes, thank you."

The Keeper gathered the two scrolls and the small stack of clay tablets. I watched him walk down the aisle, the light reflecting off the tiny bronze plates that made up his head and neck.

After my classes were over for the day, I'd made a quick trip across Jackson Square to Café Du Monde for some beignets, and

then I met up with Michel back at Presby, where he let me in
the library to do more research. It was getting late, but I wanted
to finish this new stack before I headed back to the GD.

I found a reference to an ancient Egyptian witch who untangled a curse placed on a man by the goddess Sekhmet. Every night he'd turn into a lion and devour his family. Every morning he'd awake as a man, his family alive, only to relive the nightmare all over again that night.

Poor guy, caught in some ancient, psycho version of *Groundhog Day*. I removed the scroll from beneath the translator and set it aside.

This was the second mention I'd found of a witch who could untangle a curse made by a god. It *was* possible. Now I just needed to find a present-day witch who could do the same for me. Easy, right?

The last item on the table was a round stone disk with hundreds of symbols set in a spiral pattern. I slid it under the glass and my entire body stilled as I saw the words "Athena," "temple," and "doorway" appear.

The thing was some kind of ancient manual for Athena's High Priestess. It explained how to move through this world and into the goddess's temple in Olympus so the priestesses could be initiated, bring offerings, and gain insight and instruction from Athena.

Athena's blood, kept in a small alabaster jar, was passed down from one High Priestess to the next and was used to make four symbols that if connected made the shape of a doorway.

I read the disk at least ten times, committing it to memory, finally slumping back in the chair and letting out a long breath. I stared blankly ahead of me, completely stunned as the realization set in. I'd found a way into Athena's realm.

Chills spread like lightning beneath my skin.

I needed three things to open the doorway as the High Priestesses had done. Athena's blood, the symbols committed to memory, and virginity—because every priestess of Athena's was a virgin. I had two of the three in the bag; now I just needed to figure out how to get some of Athena's blood.

By the time I left the library, it was dark outside. As soon as I cleared the double doors, I sat in the hallway and drew the symbols in my notebook exactly as they were on the disk.

Once that was done, I hurried down the steps to the first floor, but the sound of steel ringing against steel had me altering my course. Curious, I followed the noise down a hallway and into the courtyard behind the main building, where a class practiced with blades on the lawn.

I stopped next to an iron bench and watched as ten students—my age and a bit older, if I had to guess—worked. There was one girl among them, dark-haired with a fierce look of concentration.

Bran glanced over his shoulder. I lifted my hand and he walked over. "You want in? The training would do you good."

"What class is this?"

"Advanced Blades. Mostly college students. Mostly Ramseys."

I studied them, knowing that they all must be related in some way and wondering what it would be like to have such a huge family. "Any of them belong to you?" I asked.

"They are distant relations, all but the girl there. Kieran. My daughter," he said proudly. "Youngest in the class."

"That doesn't surprise me," I said, keeping the compliment tempered. Bran's ego was big enough. "How old is she?"

"Thirteen. She'd have your head separated from your body in under sixty seconds, and she could do that when she was ten."

I laughed. "I'll make sure to remember that. You don't have any other spawn lurking around Presby for me to avoid, do you?"

He lifted an eyebrow at my choice of words. "No, it's just her now."

Bran sank into silence, watching the class go through their movements. I chewed on the inside of my cheek, wondering at his meaning—if he had other children who had completed Presby and moved on or, worse, that Kieran was his only surviving child.

"Why are you here, Selkirk?"

"Just passing by. Doing some late reading."

"In the library, I gather. I hope you think hard before doing anything stupid."

I thought of the disk and swallowed. "I didn't think you cared," I joked, and then grew serious. "When I find a way to get inside Athena's temple, I'm going. Would you try and stop me?"

He thought for a long time. "Every person has a quest in life. I would not stop you from yours. A word of advice, should you find a way in: Put your emotions aside and rely on your training. You understand what I'm saying?"

"Yeah. Think with my head, not with my heart."

"Not quite. The heart is what makes a hero great. Think with your head, yes, but let your heart fill you with drive and purpose. Leave all the other crap—fears, worries—at home. Pairs!" Bran called to the group, and they broke off immediately into sparring partners. Steel against steel echoed again through the courtyard, rebounding off the buildings. "You're not ready," he continued. "You have little control over your power, and your knowledge of magic and fighting is embarrassing."

"Gee, thanks."

"You do have heart. And your ability is raw and powerful, so there is that. . . ."

"Stop," I said flatly. "I can't take the compliments. What would you do in my situation?"

"I'd make the impossible possible."

I laughed. Of course he would.

He grinned.

"Seriously, though," I prompted.

"I would do everything in me and more, Selkirk. There is power within great sacrifice, within noble deeds. There are moments . . . brief, shining moments when the impossible becomes possible. Never forget that."

He stared at the group as I gaped at him.

Who knew Bran was so deep? He wasn't just some super-jock, and I had a strong suspicion that he spoke from experience. "Okay," I said at length, "one of these days I want your story."

He snorted. "Only when you earn it, Selkirk."

Now, that was something to work toward.

By the time I made it back to the GD, I was dragging my ass.

Those beignets had been delicious, but not exactly filling. It was long past dinnertime and I was starving. I made for the kitchen. There was some bread wrapped in a towel on the counter, so I ripped off a huge chunk and then spooned out some leftover red beans and rice into a bowl.

I sat alone at the kitchen table and ate.

"Hey." Crank deposited herself across from me. "Where have you been?"

"Researching in the library," I said with my mouth full.

"You find anything?"

"Might have. . . ."

"Ari found something in the library," she told Dub as he came in rubbing his eyes and then yawning. He ignored us, opened the fridge, and seemed to stare at nothing for a long time before closing it and then sitting next to me at the table.

He scratched his head. "Fell asleep on the couch. Wondering where you were. . . ." He reached over and stole a piece of my bread.

"Stop eating my food," I said as he reached for more. "Get your own."

He sighed, laying his head on the table. "I can't. I'm too lazy."

Henri came in and slid into a chair. "So, the library, huh? What'd you find out?"

Sebastian followed a second later and leaned against the counter.

I shrugged, spooning another bite into my mouth. "I found another mention of a witch able to untangle a god's curse."

"That's good, right?" Crank said hopefully. "That means we can find one and ask her to help you."

"If that kind of witch still exists," I said. "The two mentions I've found so far have been really old. Nothing recent at all."

"I'll ask my dad about it," Sebastian offered.

"Thanks." I concentrated on getting as many red beans on

my spoon as I could. "I also found a stone disk that talked about priestesses going back and forth between our world and Athena's temple. There might be a way to open a doorway ourselves." I gave them a wry smile. "All we need is some of Athena's blood."

Henri snorted. "Sure. Simple. Let's add world peace and the discovery of life on Mars while we're at it."

I made a face at him.

"Well, since we're now on to things that will *never* happen," Dub said, leaning back in his chair and linking his hands behind his head, "let's add getting Henri to take a bath and cut his hair, and Ms. Morgan falling in love with him."

Crank giggled. "World peace might be easier."

Sebastian's quiet grin caught my eye and I smiled. Henri turned beet red and jumped up, sputtering. I laughed.

"Blow me, Dub," Henri spat, storming out of the room.

"Another thing that will never happen, Henri!" Dub called as Henri's angry footsteps thudded over the hardwood floors. The front door opened and then slammed shut.

Poor Henri. He was so in love with Ms. Morgan, the young woman who went around the GD bringing food to the kids and teaching them to read if they wanted to learn. She was, apparently, an angel. And here in the house, she was definitely Henri's Achilles' heel. No one felt bad about using it against him, either, because most of the time Henri deserved it. We all gave as good as we got. And in the end, we didn't hold grudges. We were a weird sort of family.

After I finished eating, I talked a bit with the others, cleaned up my dishes, and then went upstairs.

I sat on top of my sleeping bag and pulled out my notebook to study the symbols and wonder how in the hell I was going to get Athena's blood.

A soft knock sounded. I looked up to see Sebastian in the open doorway. "Want some company?"

"Sure."

He sat down next to me, his back against the wall, with only an inch between our shoulders. "What's that?"

"The symbols Athena's High Priestess used to open the doorway."

"Made in her blood, I take it."

"Yeah, a lot of good that does us."

I hated getting this close and then hitting a brick wall; it was frustrating as hell. How long would it take to rescue Violet and my father? And how long did they have before Athena did something irrevocable?

Sebastian slipped his hand in mine. Our fingers linked and unlinked. I liked touching him, feeling his warm skin, being connected like this. I glanced over and smiled miserably.

"What?" he asked.

His thumb made lazy strokes along the side of my hand. "You know what happens when I turn twenty-one. You know what might happen when I go after Violet and my dad." Part of me wanted to tell him to save himself the trouble of getting involved with me.

He dipped his head in agreement or in understanding, I couldn't tell which. And I couldn't help but think of Josephine's words and what exactly drew him to me. Was it me? Or was it the challenge, the rebellion, the danger involved, like she'd said?

I stared down at our hands as the silence between us stretched.

"Ari." His tone dropped low and intimate with those two syllables.

If I looked at him, he'd kiss me. I wanted that so much and yet . . .

My hand squeezed his tightly. The room grew warm. Or maybe that was just me. I swallowed and glanced up at him. Our eyes met.

The door crashed open.

Henri stood there out of breath, Dub and Crank behind him. "The Novem heirs . . . at the Saenger . . . their Mardi Gras party." He drew in a deep breath. "They caught one of Athena's minions."

Unease shot beneath my skin. I'd had firsthand encounters

with those creatures, and the memories were still fresh. But this . . . this could be the break I needed. I jumped up and started grabbing my weapons.

"They've got it in the theater?" Sebastian asked as I strapped on my blade and shoved my 9mm into the waistband of my pants. Henri nodded. Sebastian cursed softly. "Idiots."

I pulled on my jacket, then twisted the length of my hair, tied it into a knot, and secured it with two wooden hair sticks. "This is the party Gabriel was telling me about?" I finished with my hair and jerked on my boots.

"Yeah, they have it every year. Their own 'ball.' No rules. No parents."

"I thought the ruins were too dangerous."

"The Saenger is on the outskirts, like Charity Hospital. Not inside the ruins but not restored, either."

I hurried out of the room, trailing behind the others down the stairs, adrenaline starting to pump my heart faster. If we could get to this creature, get it to tell us where the gate was . . .

Crank stood with Henri and Dub at the bottom of the stairs. She was as white as a sheet, her eyes wide and unfocused. I slowed on the steps.

The ruins held all of Crank's fears. Sebastian had found her there, sitting next to the dead body of her brother, who resembled Sebastian in age and coloring. She'd been in shock. She'd thought

Sebastian was her brother, and she followed him out of the ruins and never looked back.

He never saw any need to correct her or to explain the truth.

I was of the mind that when she was ready, she'd face it. But right now, from the look on her face, there was no way in hell she was going back in there. Crank might be blocking what had happened to her brother, but she sure as hell knew what lurked in the ruins.

I went the rest of the way down, zipping up my jacket. "Dub, why don't you and Crank stay here? This shouldn't take us long."

He wanted to go. I saw it on his face—totally gung ho and revving to mix things up. Didn't matter that he was just a kid; he'd probably seen more action and horror than most cops I knew back in Memphis.

Crank remained quiet. She would never ask to stay behind. She was too proud, too stubborn, too eager to fit in with the boys.

Dub strolled to the front door and pulled it wide open. "If y'all think I'm going into the ruins at night, you're crazy."

Crank's shoulders slumped in relief, and I wanted to go right up to Dub and hug him as hard as I could. He wouldn't meet my eyes, though.

"If we're not back by morning," Sebastian said, "go find my dad."

Crank and Dub nodded.

"And stay out of my room, you big softie," Henri said, ruffling Dub's head as he walked out.

"We'll be back before you know it," I said casually, and stepped onto the porch and into the darkness of the Garden District.

I had a bad feeling about this.

TWELVE

THE THREE OF US APPROACHED THE SAENGER THEATRE FROM Canal Street. Music blared from the entrance, the bass thumping fast and thick and making my heart beat harder.

I shoved my hands into my pockets, looking up as we headed across the street. The giant alcove above the entrance was high, curved, and deep, framed with classical-style columns. Inside the alcove stood a tall statue of a naked woman—one of the muses, or maybe a goddess of some sort.

Someone had slipped a Mardi Gras mask over the statue's face and draped purple, gold, and green beads around her neck, which somehow exaggerated her nakedness and made her seem more sexual, more shameful and wicked.

That statue seemed to set the mood as we entered, passing

through the lobby to the auditorium. The balcony seating over our heads made it dark at first. Several rows of seats under the balcony provided the perfect place to make out or sit and gab with friends, but once we cleared the balcony, the place ballooned in size. It was like stepping into another world and time.

A huge bonfire burned in the middle of the theater, lighting the walls, which rose three stories high.

"Wow," I whispered, feeling as though I stood in a massive courtyard surrounded by the walls of an emperor's villa in ancient Rome.

The walls of the theater were made to resemble the exterior of temples and buildings with peaked roofs and columns. But it was all just a brilliant, beautiful illusion. What was left of the ceiling had been painted to look like the night sky, and the rest was open to the elements.

A band played on the stage, wild and extreme, with painted faces and colored hair. The loud music found its way inside me, beating through my body and making me edgy.

All the seats beyond the balcony had been removed—thousands of them, from the size and scope of the place.

Everyone danced, drank, ate, laughed, shouted, fought, kissed. The bass shook the floor. The gowns were skimpy, the masks sleek and mysterious. Everything sparkled and glowed in the firelight. It was a reckless, decadent scene, wild and carnal . . . hypnotizing.

"This way," Sebastian said, pulling me along.

We edged our way around the fire as a guy yelled to his friends, "Watch this!" He made a motion with his hands, and a flame brightened in the bonfire, elongated, and took the vague shape of a writhing woman. Someone yelled, "Make a stripper's pole!"

They all burst out laughing.

Henri led us through the crowd and around the fire until we came to the left side of the theater, where a small group stood in a circle.

I noticed Gabriel immediately. He wore a white shirt and dark pants, part of a suit that had no tie or jacket. The collar of his shirt was unbuttoned, and a plain gold mask hid half of his face.

He turned, and his eyes settled on me. Other heads turned, and I realized these were probably the Novem heirs and some of their friends. This little gathering was something for the older ones, the ones who ruled Presby and would one day be in charge of the city.

Gabriel stepped back from the circle, revealing one of Athena's grotesque creatures.

I stopped. I'd seen this kind before. One had tried to pull my skull from my spine. It looked like a human, but its limbs were gnarled, like its joints had been popped and twisted. It was hunched over and its skin was gray and leathery and hairless. An old scar ran over the corner of its left eye, forcing the eyelid partially closed. Small holes for nostrils, but no real nose to speak of. No lips, nothing to hide the rows of tiny sharp teeth that were currently bared at the onlookers.

This one was thinner and way older than the ones I'd fought at the cemetery. Weaker, which might explain how the heirs had caught it.

"I knew you'd come," Gabriel said, grinning.

Sebastian stiffened, and Henri snorted, crossing his arms over his chest.

Gabriel's eyes swept over Sebastian to Henri. From the way he glared, I'd guess that Gabriel and Henri definitely knew each other.

"We've been having some fun. Why don't you join us?"

A girl in a tight black dress and mask lifted her arms wide. A breeze blew down on us and wrapped around the creature. It screamed as some kind of invisible band tightened around it. She held it for several seconds before letting go. A guy ran into the circle with unnatural speed, a blur my eyes could hardly keep up with. Growling and screeching filled the air. Several slashes appeared on the creature's torso before the "blur" came to rest next to Gabriel.

The thing screamed and fought again as the floor buckled and broke around its feet. Roots came up like sharp stakes and impaled its foot. The music was deafening. Behind me the fire roared and the party went on, like the torture of this being didn't bother anyone.

They were playing, testing, seeing how their powers compared, what they could do. But it wasn't a fair fight. It wasn't fair at all.

I couldn't stay still. Before I even thought it through, I stepped forward and grabbed Gabriel by the arm, squeezing hard. "Tell them to stop. This isn't right."

He glanced down at my hand on his arm. Slowly, he lifted his mask. His eyes were bright and his skin was flushed. He was well on his way to being drunk. He grinned, flashing elongated teeth. His eyes swept over my neck in an obvious threat.

"Try it," I ground out.

"Oh, it wouldn't be an attempt, sweetheart. If I went for your neck, it'd be mine, trust me."

The creature screeched again, this time more desperate.

"Stop hurting it."

His brows drew together. "Why? Where's your sense of fun? That *thing* is the enemy. We are at war with Athena."

"So, what, you're going to torture it until it dies? Enemy or not, it's wrong and you know it."

Gabriel laughed. "Maybe you're feeling a little empathetic toward this creature since you're basically one and the same. Both made by Athena. Both . . . *monsters*."

My anger turned white-hot and consuming, so extreme that a weird sense of calm came in its wake. I wanted to reach for my 9mm but wasn't sure how Bloodborns or anyone here would react to that particular threat, or to being shot (if it came to that). Bloodborns stopped aging in their early twenties, when their regenerative genes took over and made them virtually immortal. Gabriel wasn't there yet, which meant if things went crazy, a bullet might kill him.

I felt it my duty to take Gabriel down a peg or two, regardless, and show his cronies that even he had weaknesses. I reached up slowly and removed the sticks from my hair.

It fell in a wave of glossy white to my waist. As expected, Gabriel's pupils dilated, glued to my hair.

And that's when I spun, grabbed his shoulder, and knocked his feet out from under him. As he fell I slid behind him, wrapping my legs around his middle and my arms around his shoulders. I shoved the sharp tips of both sticks against his jugular.

His ear was pressed against my jaw. "The only monster here is you and your sick friends," I growled. "Torturing and killing doesn't make you strong or popular, it makes you an egomaniacal

piece of shit just like Athena. You're going to let that thing go."

He squirmed. I had no idea what was happening outside my conversation, but I could feel the tension. Every kid here had some kind of power, and we were so ridiculously outnumbered that I was surprised Gabriel didn't start laughing.

"Mmm," he breathed. "Christ, your hair smells good."

The world slowed down. My body went warm and heavy, and my thoughts became unfocused. Gabriel turned in my arms, pulled me into his lap, and leaned me back in a dip. My hair slid away from my face. He smiled down at me and chuckled.

My head fell to the side, exposing my neck to him. I saw everything as if in a dream. Henri and Sebastian fought and pushed against air; Anne Hawthorne and the other girl held their hands up, palms out, somehow preventing Henri and Sebastian from getting close.

Gabriel bent down and brushed his lips against my neck. I gasped, but it came out in slow motion. "I wonder if you taste as good as you look."

His teeth grazed my skin and I shivered.

My heart pounded. My eyes latched on to the group. The flames from the bonfire flickered slowly over everything: the masks, the gowns, the revelry all around us.

And then I saw a dark shadow rising up behind Anne and the other girl. Athena's minion. It hit the girl in black. Released,

Sebastian and Henri rushed toward us, but the creature got to us first. It tore Gabriel away, grabbed my wrist, and yanked me up like a rag doll. The mesmerizing link between Gabriel and me broke instantly. The sharpness of my thoughts returned with all the ferocity of a sledgehammer at full swing.

I didn't have time to collect myself before the creature was hauling ass through the crowd, me in tow and barely able to keep up.

Screams erupted as the creature shoved people aside. Henri's shout sounded from somewhere behind me. Where the hell was Sebastian?

The creature flung students out of its path with its body and free arm. A loud explosion ripped through the theater, and a blast of hot air surged over my head. I chanced a quick glance over my shoulder to see the bonfire bursting upward as though someone had doused it with lighter fluid.

In a fraction of a second I saw Sebastian turn from the fire, eyes zeroing in on me from a ridiculous distance. Then he started after me as the creature pulled me into the lobby.

I was being dragged too fast to do anything but try to keep from falling, totally unable to reach my weapons. Pain shot through my shoulder, which was threatening to dislocate from my arm if the thing didn't release me soon.

It wasn't until we were outside and around the corner of the

theater that the creature finally stopped and let go.

I stumbled, gasping, lungs on fire as it moved away very slowly. I grabbed the hilt of the τέρας blade, and the creature's eyes followed my gesture. Neither one of us moved. It looked at me again, and this time I saw something different, something aware, intelligent, something . . . grateful?

It blinked and then dipped its head as though thanking me before taking off down South Rampart Street as Sebastian and Henri raced around the corner.

Henri kept booking after the creature. Sebastian ran past me, shouting and looking back. "You okay?!"

I nodded mutely, stunned by what had just happened but hurrying down the street after them as fast as I could. That thing was our ticket to Athena's temple; we couldn't lose it.

The only reason I caught up to Sebastian was because he had slowed. Henri was far in front of us, and the creature was putting some serious distance between itself and us.

"Henri, track it!" Sebastian yelled ahead.

Henri increased his speed, leaped into the air, and turned into a hawk.

A red-tailed hawk.

A screech blasted through the air as the bird shot upward. On the hunt.

I jogged to a stop, panting hard and bracing my hands on my

knees. "Henri's . . . a . . . hawk." I straightened and started walking in circles. Now it all made sense. His strange hazel-yellow eyes. The fact that he cleared buildings of rats and snakes for the Novem. Yeah, easy job when you're a predator. "Was anyone going to tell me?"

"It was his decision to tell. Or show. Come on, it's headed into the ruins. With Henri tracking it we can walk from here."

We headed west, away from safety and civilization and deep into the ruins of Midtown. As we walked at a fast clip my thoughts turned to Gabriel. I was so pissed that I'd allowed him to mess with me once again. I didn't know how to fight something like that or how to guard against it.

Sebastian's shoulder bumped mine. "It takes practice."

"What?"

"Learning how to block a Bloodborn's influence."

My step faltered. I caught back up to Sebastian. "I wish you would stop doing that."

"Stop doing what?"

"Reading my mind or whatever you call it."

"I'm not reading your mind. I'm reading your emotions, and it's not like I'm trying real hard. Kind of easy to put two and two together. I'd be pissed too if that happened to me."

"Yeah. Somehow I doubt you'll ever have to worry about Gabriel wanting to suck on your neck." He smiled and shrugged.

We went for a few more seconds before I said, "So how do I stop him from doing that?"

We veered off the sidewalk and around a mountain of trash and debris, and walked down the middle of the street.

"It's just a matter of being aware and knowing his intent. Gabriel's influence works because he waits until you're distracted or your guard is down. All it takes is a second. You always have to have that block in place because as soon as you don't, that's when he'll use it."

"He's such a jerk," I said, wanting to rant. "If I'm going to go all gaga for a guy, it'll be because I want to, not because some asshat is helping me along."

God, how lame was that? *Just shut up, Ari. Before you embarrass yourself even more.*

"Well, just for the record . . . forcing a girl to go *all gaga* for me isn't my style." He paused, his tone doing nothing to hide his amusement. "I like the *gaga* to be natural."

I rolled my eyes and took off at a jog before he could see that my face had gone straight past hot to volcanic.

Thirteen

Midtown looked like an old war zone.

And thirteen years ago I suppose war *had* come. In the form of wind-driven floods that used Dumpsters, vehicles, and a million other things as frontline soldiers. Some of the debris had been strong enough to take out supports and corners, collapsing parts of office buildings and high-rises. High winds had blown out windows, driving inside structures and pushing out debris.

We were entering a no-man's-land. A place Sebastian had warned me about the very first day I spent in New 2. A place you never wanted to be once the sun went down.

Yet here we were walking down the middle of South Rampart Street at night. I seriously hoped Sebastian had a plan.

"Where are we going?" I asked in a low voice, pretty sure I already knew the answer.

"Biggest part of the ruins." He nodded toward the high-rises. "We call it Center City."

"You sure that's a good idea, going into the center of the ruins?"

"We're safer in numbers. If we stay together, we should be okay. The things here are solitary hunters, and they like solitary prey. So one trying to take down two . . . it'd have to be . . ."

"What? It'd have to be what?"

"Starving."

"Oh, great. Perfect," I muttered in a slightly demented voice, eyeing the dark, vacant buildings. A shiver went down my back. "I know I'm going to regret asking, but what's out here, exactly?"

"Loups-garous, turnskins, revenants . . . Lots of things."

"I don't know what any of those things are."

He tossed me a half smile. "Loups-garous and turnskins are shape-shifters who've gone wild. Feral. They no longer recognize anything from their human life. They'd hunt their own family if they could. 'Revenant' is a French word. It means returning, like returning from the dead—"

I grabbed Sebastian's arm and stopped dead in the street. "Wait a minute. Are you talking about corpses walking around undead, like zombies?"

"Yes and no." He seemed very quiet and completely in tune with everything around us. "Call it whatever you want, I guess. Revenants are more than undead humans. They're soulless vampires. And before you say vampires don't have souls, that's a myth. Me, my mother, my grandmother, Gabriel . . . we all have souls. We were all born into this world just like humans. And the humans who are Turned, they keep their souls too; they just awake changed as a Dayborn vampire."

"So how does a vampire lose its soul and become a revenant?"

"It happens when a vampire Turning a human screws up. If the person dies during the blood exchange, they end up reviving without a soul, and without it, they aren't . . . right, you know? That's why the Novem has strict rules about Turning humans. Taking a person to the brink of death, doing the blood exchange *before* their soul leaves their body, is an exact science. Revenants are usually a result of amateurs."

"So why not kill them right away, when they realize?"

He was quiet for a moment as we turned onto Girod Street. Ahead, tall gray skyscrapers rose into the night sky, windows blown out, skeletons of their former selves. Our footsteps were loud, crunching over layers of debris and passing rotted-out vehicles and things that didn't belong—a bathtub, a lone carousel horse lying on its side, a pontoon boat. . . .

"Imagine wanting to save someone you love," he said.

"Or Turning someone you love so they won't grow old, so you won't lose them. And it comes out wrong. How can you kill them? How can you douse them with gasoline and light them on fire? Because that's the only way to completely kill them once they've risen. So their makers let them go. But like I said, the Novem is pretty strict, so there aren't too many of them around."

The area was so still that any noise, any occasional shuffle or metallic creak, was like thunder. Sebastian's words were oddly depressing. There was humanity even in the creation of the walking dead. Loss. Regret. Love.

"When is the Novem going to clean up this place?"

"Who knows. Maybe never. They'll restore the GD before they'll ever get to this place. They send out executioners every once in a while to keep the ruins from becoming overrun, but other than that, they leave it alone."

The street up ahead was blocked with a huge rubble pile. One side of a building had collapsed in the street, making a barrier of rebar, concrete, and glass.

"Be careful of glass and metal," Sebastian said as we climbed over the pile at the lowest point. Everything in the ruins smelled like concrete dust and damp rot. The scent was thick and it stuck in the back of my throat. No matter how many times I swallowed, it wouldn't go away.

The cry of the hawk echoed suddenly. "This way," Sebastian said.

Once we made it over the debris, we crossed into the intersection with Loyola.

The hairs on the back of my neck stood up.

From the blackness of the ruins we were being watched. Out in the open we were moving targets. Everywhere, on either side of us and above us in the tall buildings, it felt like a thousand eyes were upon us.

I turned slowly in a circle, gazing up the tall buildings of Entergy Tower and the Hyatt Regency, behind which was the Superdome.

My hand fell back onto the grip of my 9mm; curling my fingers around the cool material gave me a sense of calm. Every once in a while we heard noises, scrapes of metal, thuds, and scramblings.

"They're following us," I whispered, knocking shoulders with Sebastian as we crossed the street. "Why aren't they attacking? And why the hell didn't you bring a flamethrower?"

I wasn't being funny—I was being desperate. How were we supposed to fight something that didn't die until it was burned to ashes? We headed for Entergy Tower. It rose up from a base of debris, and most of the twenty-eight floors were open to the elements.

"Don't run yet," Sebastian said. "Just keep walking like you are. They might hesitate long enough for us to make it inside. If they attack, though, we run like hell."

My skin was crawling. I didn't like this, didn't like being out in the open. My heart was pounding. I was sweating even though it wasn't warm.

As we approached the tower, the hawk swooped down and materialized into Henri. He hadn't even broken his movement, just fell into step next to Sebastian and immediately began giving us the stats. "Doorway is inside Entergy Tower. Eighteenth floor. East face. I was able to barricade the thing in a closet before he could disappear. It won't hold him for long." Our pace had picked up. "There are two turnskins, one near the Hyatt, the other near the rubble pile." Okay, that wasn't too bad, we could— "Three revenants. One in the parking deck, another on the roof of the tower, and the third one is coming up behind us!"

Henri turned just as the creature collided with him. He rolled onto his back, using the momentum to flip the revenant over him, sending it flying.

The brief flash I got of the thing—ragged clothes; sallow, sunken skin; matted hair; sharp teeth—was terrifying.

"Shit," Sebastian cursed.

"Hurry!" Henri ran toward the tower.

I pulled my gun, cradling it in my hand. A wolf dropped down in front of me, a snarling, rangy thing. I fired. It yelped and went back a few steps as I tossed the gun to my left hand and pulled the τέρας blade out with my right, swinging it in an arc as the wolf charged again.

The wolf came so close I could smell its rotten breath. The blade cut through skin and muscle. It all happened so fast. I didn't think, just reacted.

We moved in a pack of three, constantly turning and watching. The entrance to the tower was only steps away. "I thought you said the Novem keeps the numbers down and these things hunt alone," I whispered fiercely to Sebastian.

"They do. Normally. They must be hungry." A large black panther darted from the rubble pile, bounded across the street, leaped onto the top of a hollowed-out car, and pushed off toward us.

"Got it!" Sebastian lifted his hands and made a big sweeping motion, turning his body in a circle. Wind picked up. Nearby, a car without doors or windows lifted as if caught in the swirl of Sebastian's movement. The car spun toward the cat, enveloping the animal inside the frame, and then crashed into the side of a nearby building.

"Inside!" Henri held the door open and we raced into the building and up the stairwell. By the fourth floor we heard a

bang from below as something or some*things* gave chase.

Great. Just fourteen more floors to go.

By the time we hit the tenth, my legs and my lungs were burning and I was using the railing to pull some of my weight. Still we pushed on. From the sounds below us I knew the creatures were closing in, and I had no idea what would happen when we made it to the eighteenth floor. All I cared about was beating them to the doorway.

We finally made it. Sebastian ushered us through and then grabbed an old metal chair and stuck one of its legs through the door handle. It wouldn't hold them for long, but maybe long enough. . . .

"Where's the doorway?" I asked Henri.

"This way."

We ran down the hallway to the sound of the wind moaning through the building. Fear slid into my psyche. I was not a fan of heights. The idea that we were in a structure this high and the outer walls were completely gone . . . I shuddered just thinking about it.

After a few turns down a hallway, we came into a large office. Wind blew in hard—easy since the entire far wall was *gone.* In the distance the lights of the French Quarter shone and sparkled with life. A piece of rebar was shoved between the metal handles of a closet that was currently taking a massive pounding. The

hinges on one door were separating from the wall. Athena's minion would be out soon.

"It's in this wall, I think, the gateway. See the four symbols?" Henri said, out of breath.

I edged closer to the wall on my left to see four symbols marked in dried blood, which if connected made a large rectangle.

I turned my attention back to the closet. I needed that creature in order to find out where the doorway led and what awaited us on the other side. "Once we let it out, can you guys hold it?"

Blue light appeared over Sebastian's hands as he and Henri faced the closet. They both nodded. At least they appeared confident. I, on the other hand, not so much. Hell, the thing might not even be able to communicate with us.

"Shit," Henri said suddenly, turning around to face the missing wall.

A head, upside down, looked in with feverish eyes. The revenant from the roof had scurried down the side of the tower. It crawled inside and across the ceiling before dropping down in front of us.

We backed up, moving slowly toward the wall with the symbols. The minion continued to pound on the closet door, about to blow it clean off the wall. Another revenant burst into the room, and even though I knew my weapon wouldn't stop it, I pulled my gun and fired on instinct.

The revenants rushed us just as Athena's minion broke through the closet door, charged behind us, and disappeared into the wall with the symbols.

Henri jumped in front of us, throwing his arms wide and running right at the revenants. "I got this!" he shouted. He slammed into the creatures, digging in his heels and pushing them back.

Oh God, they were headed toward the missing wall! I screamed as Henri shoved them, himself included, out of the office and into midair.

"Henri!" I ran forward, my fear of heights dropping me to my belly. I shimmied toward the edge. *Oh God, oh God, oh God . . .*

Wind roared and blasted against me, sending my loose hair flying straight up. I watched them fall in a tumble of limbs, grappling each other, trying to hold on and take Henri down with them. My fingers curled around the edges of the floor. Glass punctured my palms.

End over end they tumbled. The momentum finally broke one of the revenants off, but the other one held on to Henri like glue.

C'mon, Henri . . .

Henri shifted from human to hawk, slipping from the revenant's flailing grasp. His wings shot out, caught air, and he banked right, soaring out over the city below and leaving the revenant with a tail feather clutched between two outstretched fingers.

I turned away before it hit the ground, focusing on Henri as he glided toward the lights of the Quarter.

"Guess that's one way to clear a room."

I rose onto my elbows at Sebastian's dry remark. He was shaking his head and wearing a lopsided smile.

"You're insane. *Henri* is insane." I scooted far back from the edge before getting to my feet. I trembled from head to toe.

"I would say 'Welcome to New 2,' but I think you've already heard that one. Here, let me see." Sebastian stepped closer and grabbed my hand, turning it palm up.

The only sound now was the wind crying through the dark building. It blew around us, sending my hair flying in all directions as Sebastian pulled a shard of glass from my palm. Blood oozed from the wound, a shining ruby in a scene of black, gray, and white.

Sebastian's hand tightened on mine.

We looked up in realization at the same time. His gray eyes flared to silver.

I didn't breathe.

It was easy to forget sometimes that Sebastian was the child of a Bloodborn vampire. He'd once told me that blood was hard to resist for any of his kind. It didn't mean he'd ever take it, but one thing I knew for sure: If he did, he'd become a blood-drinker from that day forward. An Arnaud, like Josephine, and that was something Sebastian never wanted.

He closed my hand, stepped back, and then walked around me to the wall with the blood symbols.

A long shaky exhale flowed between my lips.

"Ari, look." I moved to stand next to him and drew up short. His hand was *in* the wall. "It works."

I grabbed his arm and jerked his hand back. "We don't know what's on the other side."

"Ari . . ."

"I . . . I don't know what to do," I confessed. "What should we—" Indecision gripped me. My father and Violet were probably beyond that doorway. The minion might be on its way to tell Athena.

"Ari."

A chill slid down my spine at the warning tone in his voice. Sebastian faced away from the wall. His palm was up and a blue light was already forming.

Another revenant stood in the room.

It lunged just as a turnskin leaped through the office door. I stepped back, stumbling on debris as blue light filled the room. My arms pinwheeled as I fell backward. Oh God. Not backward! I screamed.

Sebastian spun and reached for me, but it was too late. I was falling through Athena's doorway.

FOURTEEN

PANIC AND SHOCK ROLLED OVER ME. IT WAS TOO SOON. I WASN'T prepared, had yet to master my power. . . .

I landed hard on my back, my elbows taking the brunt of the fall and stinging with a painful vibration. Heat, voices, and music brushed past my senses, but before I could figure them out, Sebastian fell through the gate, tripping over me.

My gaze followed his path as he slid to a stop in front of an enormous hall filled with feasting people and creatures, all looking our way.

It felt like every bit of blood drained from my veins, leaving ice water in its place. I looked around the hall. No one got up or stopped eating, but the way they watched made my insides shrivel.

Massive Greek columns lined the long sides of the room. Beyond the right row of columns were steps leading to a garden. Fires burned in stone bowls around the outer edges of the room. Tables formed a large open-ended rectangle, and in the spacious center of the room was a small inground pool, its sides raised to the height of a low stone bench, low enough for me to see smooth, dark water and the flames of the fires reflecting off its surface.

The tables were piled high with everything you'd expect from an ancient feast, yet there were also plates full of French fries, chips, cookies, and pizza.

Servants filled glasses and replaced empty platters with more food.

I glanced behind me to see guards on either side of the doorway we'd come through. It was a plain marble wall with dried-blood symbols at four corners, and it had been carved to resemble an actual door. To the right of the wall was a large alcove containing a marble statue of a man—a huge, bearded man—with a shocked, angry expression and outstretched arms. His hands were missing, and the sight immediately made me think of the stone hands holding the infant in the library back at Presby.

Sebastian reached out and grabbed my hand. We stood together. The beings here were varied, and it was hard to tell just by looking who was human, witch, vampire, or demigod. But it

was easy to pick out the nightmares, the grotesque witches, the leathery gray minions, a few harpies. . . .

But there was really only one person here who mattered.

Athena sat at the far end of the room, facing us. Her feet were propped up on the table. A small grin appeared at the corner of her mouth before she bit into the round piece of fruit she held in her hand. Behind her, set against the wall, was a raised platform with three thrones, the biggest in the middle.

Her eyes met mine with mirth and satisfaction.

She swallowed her bite, and then her full lips drew back to reveal perfect white teeth. Her booted feet slid off the table. The beings in the room turned to watch as she stepped onto the table and hopped down to the floor on the other side, striding toward us with a victorious gleam in her shining emerald eyes.

Her black hair was down in long, loose strands and thin braids decorated with bone beads and strips of leather. She wore a skintight black bodysuit. The light danced off the leather, revealing scales of some sort. No doubt another suit made from a once-living creature—or one that still lived in some way. The last one she wore moved around her body like a living parasite.

A shudder ripped through me.

Athena was gorgeous. Tall, stacked, and flawless. Perfect in every way on the outside, but on the inside she was ugly as sin. Rotted. Demented. Evil.

"I see you brought the Lamarliere brat." She stopped in front of him, giving him a thorough perusal. "You look just like your father."

I didn't want her talking to him or noticing him in any way. The fact that he was here with me spelled disaster. Athena would use him in a heartbeat to mess with me. "Where's Violet?" I asked.

She turned, studying me with a calculating look. "Violet. Intriguing little thing, isn't she? Different. Like you. Tell me, Ari, did you really think you could come into my realm and take her back? That you could defeat *me*?"

"I did it once."

"No," she shot back immediately, leaning closer. "The Novem did, and only because I let them. But they're not here now, are they?" She straightened. "I like Violet. I think I might keep her, groom her, influence her. . . . These are her formative years, after all."

She was trying to bait me, prove that she was in control and I was nothing but an insignificant toy she could play with.

"Let Violet and my father go back with Sebastian, and I'm yours," I said. "I'll do whatever you want."

I refused to meet the stunned gaze Sebastian was giving me. This was, and had always been, between me and Athena.

Athena leaned in. "A little news flash for you. You're mine already."

The sound of chains across stone echoed through the temple.

The guests sat straighter. The grin that passed over Athena's face made the hairs on my body rise. "Perfect." She made a gesture toward the sound of the chains. "I give to you the mighty Theron!" she yelled to the crowd. They cheered and banged on the tables as she turned back to me with a smirk. "The evening's entertainment has arrived."

Two of Athena's minions dragged a man by his armpits over the mosaic tiles. His legs were loosely shackled together and his feet slid limply along the floor. His head hung low. He wore black boxer briefs and nothing else. Patches of puckered red and pink skin—new scars—covered his sallow skin.

As they drew closer my gut started to twist in a slow knot. Damp blond hair stuck to his neck and face. He glanced up, his eyes burning hatred at Athena. And then they saw me and widened.

Oh God. I knew who it was. I'd never seen his face before, but I knew. I knew . . .

My father.

Instant tears shot to my eyes. I rushed past Athena, but she grabbed the back of my shirt and jerked me into her. One arm wrapped around my waist and the other came across my chest. Guards seized Sebastian's hands before he could make a move against her. She held me, whispering in my ear as my heart pounded wildly.

"You cannot save him, Ari. Nothing can save someone who has betrayed me so completely."

My father struggled, but he was so weak his attempt did little to stop the guards from forcing him down toward the pool. My mind raced, a chaos of so many thoughts that I didn't know what to do.

Athena released me and clapped. "Menai!"

A young woman stood from her seat at the end of one of the long tables. She was tall and slim, oozing boredom and confidence. She had deep red hair that fell in long waves and wore brown suede boots laced to just below her knees and a short skirt to match. A bow was secured on her back, the string crossing over her chest.

"These two are yours to watch," Athena told her, and then strode back to her seat.

The two guards by the gate stepped away from the wall and shoved us toward the archer as she went back to the table and made room on the long bench.

I sat down numbly, between Sebastian and Menai.

The guards backed away but remained standing behind us. Menai began piling her plate with food. "Might as well eat," she said, looking at me through earthy green eyes. "This might be the only time she feeds you."

Sheer terror had a hold on me as my gaze went to my father. "What are they going to do to him?"

"Throw him in the pool." She tore off a large chunk of bread and shoved the entire thing into her mouth. "Just like last night and the night before." She eyed the water, chewing and not looking at me when she said, "I suggest you stay in your seat. You get up, you try to help him, and she'll kill him, understand?"

Athena jumped onto her table, stepped over the food, and plopped back down in her chair, putting her feet up. She never even glanced at my father; her eyes were on me the entire time.

The guards unshackled my father and shoved him in the water, ignoring his raw, desperate pleading.

The splash reverberated off the walls. Everyone held their breath.

The water rippled. My father's head emerged. I grabbed the edge of the table and squeezed tightly. He made one stroke toward the edge of the pool before he screamed.

Panic flared, making it hard for me to breathe.

WHAT THE HELL IS IN THE WATER?! my mind screamed over and over.

The music started again, hard and pounding. A tail flopped in the water. The assembly cheered as over and over again my father screamed and choked on bloody water.

I surged up, but only made it an inch or two before Sebastian's hand clamped hard over my thigh, his other hand coming across to hold my arm. A roar built in my throat. Up, I wanted up!

Oh my God, I need up. . . . Tears streamed down my face. "Let me go."

"You can't help him," he said. "Athena is waiting for you to run to him, Ari. Look at her. Ari. *Look* at her."

I blinked, tears dropping off my chin onto the table, and turned my head in Athena's direction. One raven eyebrow quirked up. She bit into her fruit, chewing and then smiling brightly.

My father's screams echoed through the temple and into every crevice of my being. The smell of food became disgusting. I was going to be sick.

Menai continued to eat, her gaze on my father but her voice low. "Athena learned this bit of torture from the Romans. Moray eels. Flesh eaters. Especially brutal since they have a second jaw. Big jaw clamps down. Little jaw comes out, bites, and rips off flesh."

My vision went blurry with shock and tears. "Shut up," I forced out through gritted teeth. One of my father's arms hung over the edge off the pool, but it was limp, his fingers twitching. . . .

"Theron is immortal. Unfortunately for him, he'll live, repair somewhat, and be ready for more by tomorrow night."

My nails dug deeper into the table, leaving impressions in the wood. "Shut up."

"Like I said, you better eat now while you can. Might be you in that pool tomorrow. . . ."

Blinding rage ripped through my last shred of tolerance. "SHUT UP!"

My pulse beat out of control, so loud and fast through my eardrums, it drowned out the screaming and the cheers and the music. I moved without premeditation, hand snaking out, grabbing the fork by my plate, and shoving it into Menai's hand, stabbing with as much force as I possessed in my body.

It pinned her hand to the table.

She shrieked, turned, and gripped me by the neck with her free hand. I kept my hold on the fork and jerked my other hand from Sebastian's, propelled by frustration, fear, and fury. I grabbed her by the throat. Fat teardrops fell from my eyes. I couldn't breathe, but I didn't care.

Menai's face turned red. Her eyes bugged out. Veins enlarged along her temple and under the thin skin below her eyes. No one moved to help her. I heard laughter and shouts of encouragement thrown Menai's way. They thought this was funny.

I squeezed harder. She squeezed back.

I felt it, the stirring of something monstrous inside me waking, uncoiling, hissing through my mind. My power shot down my arm and out my hand, the force of it surprising me and causing me to break contact. She followed my lead, both of us dropping back and gasping for air. I caught a glimpse of her neck as a faint trace of white disappeared back into a normal, fleshy color before her hand went to her throat, her eyes wide in surprise.

Somewhere in the rush of blood to my brain, I became aware of Sebastian tugging me back, speaking to me, but I couldn't hear what he said. I blinked rapidly, trying to regain control. *Breathe. In and out.*

Finally, my vision sharpened.

The guards pulled my father from the now red water and left him on the floor.

Oh God. His body was torn—

I turned in the space between me and the archer and puked on the pretty mosaic tiles.

I stayed bent far over the bench, gasping as my stomach curled into a tight, sickening ball. Nothing, no amount of abuse in my childhood, could've prepared me for this kind of torture. I thought I'd seen my share of brutality, but this . . . this was beyond comprehension.

A napkin hit me on the side of my face. I glanced up as Menai turned away and resumed eating. I wiped my face, drew in several deep breaths, and tried like hell to regain my composure before I straightened. I almost laughed because the idea of even trying to be composed was a joke. Not here. Not when my father had been left on the floor in a pool of blood and hanging flesh while everyone ate and laughed.

Sebastian's hands were on my arm. "Ari," he said, leaning

close to me. "Let me help you." His gray eyes swirled with concern. His skin had gone a few shades paler, and his dark lips were drawn in a tight line.

My throat hurt. I couldn't speak.

"Let me calm you," he said.

Sebastian had the ability to mesmerize, to put people into a trancelike state. He'd done it to the two clerks when we'd accessed my birth records at Charity Hospital.

Weariness settled over me, weighing me down. Was it weak to want that? To want a lessening of this horror and pain? He wiped his thumb through the hot trail of tears running down my face. And for the first time in years I wanted to retreat to my safe spot, to that inner space inside me where I'd gone as a child. A place where no matter what was done to me on the outside, nothing could reach me in my dark little corner.

He tipped my chin so I'd look at him. His eyes were glassy as we stared at each other. I nodded, accepting help, admitting defeat. I'd never opened myself up to that with anyone else.

"Touching," Athena said, interrupting.

My eyelids slid slowly closed as the dull realization of what we'd just done settled like a two-ton brick in my gut. *No, no, no . . .* Hopelessness erased any fight I had left. We'd just shown her something else she could use to hurt us.

Her hands were on her hips, but this time, as I expected, her gaze was not on me but Sebastian. Thoughtful, scheming, deciding. She grabbed Sebastian's arm and hauled him to his feet.

He was just a hair taller than Athena, and together they looked oddly similar with their black hair and perfect skin. She leaned close to him. "Tell me, Mistborn, have you taken blood yet?"

Her fingers trailed along his jaw; it flexed beneath her touch. All my anger returned in a dizzying flash. Sebastian held her gaze with a hard glare. He didn't answer.

"You haven't, have you?" She leaned even closer, brushing her cheek against his, then drawing back, retracing the path of her cheek with her lips this time. "You smell innocent. How . . . wonderful." She turned to the guards, the same ones with the blood of my father on their hands. "Take them back."

"What?" I rasped.

"You're going back to New 2. The doorway will be sealed behind you."

All I wanted was to get out of this nightmare, and yet I struggled against the guards as they grabbed me. "No!"

"I'll admit I didn't expect you to come tumbling through the gate, but your timing was perfect. Hard to leave now, isn't it? Now that you know what I've been doing to dear ol' Daddy." She went from maniacal to brutal in a flash, grabbing me by the chin and forcing me to look at her closely. "This is my realm. My time. My decisions. I deal with you when I see fit." Her nose brushed mine. "Remember who's really in control, gorgon."

"Why don't you just kill me and get it over with," I cried.

"Please." She laughed, but her words came out in a snarl. "I haven't had this much fun in at least a century and—"

"Let them go. My father is of no use to you. And Violet, she's just a kid."

"So are you, my dear." She shoved me back into the arms of the guards. "Enjoy stewing in your thoughts and worries, Aristanae. Try not to have too many nightmares thinking of all the fun we're having here without you."

The guards yanked me back toward the gate. "No!" I kicked out and screamed, but none of it mattered. We were going back.

Because Athena wanted me to suffer.

FIFTEEN

SEBASTIAN AND I WERE SHOVED THROUGH THE DOORWAY SO hard, we came through sliding on our hands and knees, landing at the feet of Michel, Henri, Bran, and Josephine.

My chin hit the floor, splitting the skin. Glass stuck into my palms and knees, but the pain was nothing compared to the desolation inside. I stared at Josephine's expensive-looking black heels, feeling like I was there but not there—still immersed in the horror of Athena's temple.

"*Merde*," Josephine sighed annoyingly. "Bleed on someone else's shoes." She lifted her foot, prepared to push my face away with the sole of her high heel.

"Lay off, Grandmère," Sebastian said coldly.

"The gate has closed," Michel said, interrupting Josephine's reply. He stepped forward as I pushed slowly and painfully to a sitting position. A glance over my shoulder told me he was right; his hands pressed flat against the wall. Athena had sealed it from the other side.

"On your feet, Selkirk." Bran's gruff voice drew my attention. He leaned over, hand outstretched, his face trying to be all fierce and grim, but there was only concern written on his features. He was actually—wonders never ceased—worried. "Stop looking at me like that," he growled. "Take my hand and stand like a warrior, damn it."

Fresh tears blurred my vision, and my throat closed. I did as he demanded, wincing as glass pressed farther into my skin.

Michel grabbed Sebastian's face gently, his expression fierce and stark. "You are . . . unhurt?"

"Yes, Father."

A long string of relieved mutterings—prayers of thanks and what sounded like a few curses—fell from Michel as he gathered his son into a hug and held him tightly.

An odd stirring of loneliness went through me. Sebastian rolled his eyes, but I could tell he welcomed the embrace. The smile I returned wasn't heartfelt. It hurt.

I turned away, bit my lip, and yanked the shard of glass from my palm.

"Here." Bran stood in front of me and shoved a wad of

balled-up old printer paper into my bleeding hand. "Hold on to that for now."

"Thanks."

"Physical pain," he said quietly, "has a way of lessening . . . other pains."

I lifted my head in surprise. Bran understood far better than I'd thought. I'd take physical pain over internal pain any day.

"I take it you saw your father?"

I dropped my gaze and managed a nod.

"Come, Ari," Michel said, walking toward the office doorway. "A warm meal, a hot shower, and rest await you."

"And then we will discuss your little . . . adventure," Josephine promised.

Michel gave me the same room I'd used once before, after escaping with him from Athena's prison. I showered on autopilot, redressed, and then wiped the steam from the mirror to stare at what was reflected there.

The cut on my chin was red and vivid against the paleness of my skin and hair. Faint mauve-blue shadows curved under eyes that looked weary, lost, and hollow. Yes, so hollow.

After a deep exhale I straightened and went in search of the others, even though all I really wanted to do was crawl under the clean comforter, close my eyes, and sink into oblivion.

I found them on the second-story balcony overlooking the courtyard. Lanterns on the walls provided a soft yellow glow. Potted ferns and other plants made the wide space feel homier. I stepped outside into the cool air and the sounds of conversation.

Bran leaned back against the railing with his arms crossed over his chest. Michel and Josephine sat on wicker chairs as the butler set drinks on the table. Sebastian was sitting on the end of a chaise lounge, his arms resting over his knees. He lifted his head at my approach, a strand of wet hair falling over his eye. He raked his fingers through it as he sat straighter.

I didn't have the strength to distance myself from my emotions and tell them what had happened in Athena's temple. It was all too fresh.

"Sebastian has filled us in," Michel said with sympathy. He cleared his throat. "Had I known Theron would suffer so greatly, I would not have prevented you from freeing him when we escaped Athena's prison."

That was another memory I really didn't want to remember, yet there it was, staring me in the face. I'd freed everyone in that prison except my father. He had hunted and killed who knew how many beings on Athena's behalf. He was an enemy to the Novem, a Son of Perseus who had loved my mother so deeply that he had betrayed the goddess. And I could have set him free.

"You're not responsible, Michel," I said without a trace of

emotion. Michel had been in Athena's prison for a decade, and—who knows—my father might've been the one who put him there.

"I find it very hard to believe she would simply send you both back unharmed," Josephine said.

"And I couldn't care less," I said tiredly, "about setting your mind at ease, Josephine."

"Why, you belligerent little—"

"Did she bargain?" Bran cut in, glaring at Josephine. "Did she say what she wanted?"

"For me to suffer until I break, at which point I'm sure she'll kill my father and Violet—probably make me watch—and then she'll kill me. I really don't see what's left to talk about. I'm going home."

I walked away, heading through the house and out into the night air. I moved like a ghost, letting my memory guide me through the streets.

And then I was home in my room toeing off my boots, removing my weapons, sliding fully dressed beneath the sleeping bag, pulling it to my chin, and finally shutting out the world.

The sound of drums echoed through the house, vibrating the walls and coming up through the floor and into my body to shake me awake. I rolled onto my back, keeping my eyes closed and letting the beat pound through me. It was like waking to a morning thunderstorm—one of my favorite things. Except it didn't bring me joy. Not this time.

I stayed still for a while, listening, letting my muscles relax and sink farther into the weighted sensation of exhaustion and defeat. My pulse seemed to keep time with the beat—deep and constant and full of pain.

"Gah. It's too early in the morning for that shit," a voice groaned within my room, and a fist hit the wall halfheartedly.

I turned to see Dub grabbing his sleeping bag and pulling it over his head. And then on my other side Crank was yawning and stretching her arms high into the air. I sat up, rubbing my eyes.

"Morning, Ari." Crank scratched her nose. She looked puffy and very young from sleep. Her braids were bent and several wisps of hair had come free.

"What are you guys doing in here?"

Dub muttered under the sleeping bag.

"They call it moral support." Henri's sleep-deepened voice came from across the room. He sat up, and his red hair fell around his face, loose from its band. He ran a hand down his scruffy face and then met my stare with a quiet intensity. "It was their idea, not mine."

I didn't know how to respond, so I watched as he got up, tossed his sleeping bag over his shoulder, and shuffled out of the room.

I hadn't heard anyone come in last night. *Moral support,* I thought. My gaze fell on the empty sleeping bag across the room.

"Bastian slept here too," Crank said, getting up and readjusting her overall straps. I wondered if she ever took them off. Then she stilled and worry came into her eyes. "I'm sorry about your dad. Will we ever get them back, you think?"

My father, I wasn't sure. Not after witnessing what Athena was doing to him. I had no clue how to save him and I had no idea where Violet was being held. I only knew she was missing from the sleepover in my room, and we wouldn't be complete until—

"Ari?" Crank asked slowly. "What's wrong?"

I blinked. My entire body hummed like it was one gigantic goose bump. I couldn't believe it; it'd been staring me right in the face all this time. "Crank. The laundry."

We had a laundry room downstairs with an old machine that Crank had fixed. I'd taken a basket down with my dirty clothes a few days ago and hadn't washed them yet.

"Huh?"

"Please tell me no one has thrown my clothes in the laundry."

"No, we all do our own. Ari, you look weird."

Sebastian appeared in the doorway, his hair damp with sweat, still clutching his drumsticks.

"You felt her go all weird, didn't you, Bas," Crank asked.

And then I was up, darting past Sebastian and practically flying down the curving staircase. Footsteps echoed behind. I leaped over the final three steps and rounded the corner, my socked feet sliding on the hardwood. I swung into the laundry room.

There. My basket. My hands were shaking. I threw my clothes out, looking, looking. . . . I froze.

My shirt. The shirt I was wearing the day Violet disappeared.

I picked it up, heart pounding, seeing the memory so clearly in my mind of Violet leaping onto Athena's back and shoving her dagger into the goddess's chest. They'd disappeared and the dagger had dropped to the ground. The same dagger I'd picked up. The one covered with Athena's blood. The one I'd wiped clean using the end of my shirt.

I turned to see my friends crowded in the threshold. I lifted the shirt, shocked. "Athena's blood opens the doorway."

SIXTEEN

"I'M *GOING.*" DUB CROSSED HIS ARMS STUBBORNLY OVER HIS CHEST.

I frowned at him and said for the hundredth time, "You're not going."

"Well, if he goes, then I go," Crank said.

"Crank," I said, "Dub is not going. And neither are you."

We'd gathered around the coffee table in the living room, and the resulting conversation was giving me a tension headache behind my left eye.

"You guys," I said tiredly, "I have no idea if this will even work."

"Well, why would you want it to?" Henri asked. "You'll just end up right back in Athena's hall."

"No, I don't think so. The instructions I found are to Athena's old temple, back before she killed Zeus and took his temple as her own. Everything I've learned so far says that she abandoned her temple for Zeus's, and that's the one Sebastian and I were in."

"But there's no way of knowing what awaits us in her old temple either," Sebastian pointed out.

"I know, but it's our only alternative. Athena closed the gate we found in the ruins, so even if we wanted to use that one, we couldn't. She won't be expecting us to come back. She thinks we're on her time, at her mercy. And if her old temple is in the same realm and abandoned, like the history books say, then we might have a shot." I rubbed a hand down my face. "I get that there are a ton of things I don't know about the doorways, or gates, or whatever the hell they're called. But I still have to try."

Sebastian and I stared at one another for a long moment before he turned his attention to Crank and Dub. "We'll make the symbols away from the house, in the cemetery. We'll pack food and water and weapons."

Dub started to complain.

"Dub. It's too dangerous," I interrupted. "End of story."

"You know me and Crank can take care of ourselves."

"I know that. Taking care of yourselves is one thing, but entering the realm of a goddess is another. I can't worry about Athena getting ahold of you. I can't be constantly checking on you, looking over my shoulder . . . those things could get us killed. And it's not because I think you need babysitting—it's because I care. A lot. So just, please, don't give me a hard time about this. Please stay so I know at least you two are safe. Let me worry about Violet, okay?"

I hadn't meant to go on like that or get into my feelings. For a moment no one responded.

"I have an extra sheath you can borrow," Dub offered, finally giving up.

I relaxed. The fight was over. Thank God.

"And I found a box of ammo a while back. Not sure if they're the right kind of bullets for your gun, but you can have them if you want," Crank said.

"Sneaking in, just the three of us, without an army or a bunch of Novem heads," Henri contemplated. "I like it. We can move faster and not worry about egos and everyone fighting about who's in charge."

"Oh, I almost forgot!" Crank got off her chair and yelled behind her as she jogged from the room. "Stay there! I have a surprise!"

She banged around the kitchen and then returned with . . . a cake? She set it down on the coffee table and handed us forks. I pretended not to notice her shaking hands. "You know what a king cake is, right, Ari?"

"I know there's a plastic baby in it, but that's about it," I answered, hoping that Crank wasn't losing it. She was extremely worried. We were leaving and our chances were one in a million. If Crank wanted to have cake, we'd have cake.

"It's twisted deep-fried dough with cream cheese filling. Trust me, you'll like it."

There was icing poured and hardened on the top, and sections were colored purple, green, and gold.

"Where'd you get it?" I asked, taking a slice and shoving a bite into my mouth.

"Perks of running the mail," Crank said. "I smell cake and the box mysteriously never gets delivered."

I laughed. "You stole it."

"Hell yeah, I did. It was addressed to the Pontalba apartments."

Which for us was enough said. Everyone knew that Novem families lived in those swanky apartments. And they sure as hell wouldn't miss a king cake.

"Right on," Dub said, clinking forks with Crank like a toast, his cheeks filled like a chipmunk's.

Henri found the baby, so it was his responsibility, they all said, to find a cake next year. And I damn sure would do everything in my power to make sure there would *be* a next year.

Crank drove us the four blocks to Lafayette Cemetery. We could've walked, but she insisted, saying we shouldn't tire ourselves out. She parked on the curb. We slid the rear door up and jumped out.

We headed down the first row of tombs, then the second. "How about that one there?" Dub pointed to an intact tomb at the far end of the row. It had roughened marble sides and was big enough to make the doorway.

"Perfect. Let's use the other side, though, since it's hidden from the main gate," I said.

Once we were there, I let my heavy backpack slide off my shoulders and placed the small plastic container I carried on a flat bit of stone nearby. While the boys had packed the bags and weapons, Crank and I had used as little water as possible to wet the stiff blood from my shirt and squeeze it into the container. It was Athena's blood for sure, but watered down.

Dub handed me my notebook with the symbols. "We can each do one," he said.

"No. It has to be me. The tablet said it has to be done by a woman in order to work." My cheeks turned hot and I kept the whole virginity thing to myself. "Once it's made, though, anyone should be able to go through."

Sebastian and Henri brushed off the spots where I'd make the drawings.

After they were done, I took the container and dipped my finger in the blood. I drew each symbol slowly and perfectly, referencing my sketches from the notebook. The watered-down blood was so light, I wasn't sure it'd work, so I waited for the symbols to dry and then did another coat.

Four coats later I stood back. The wall looked like the wall in Entergy Tower, though not exactly. The symbols were slightly different.

I set the container down, used a bottle of water to rinse my hands, and took a deep breath as the guys stood in front of the wall trying to note any energy disturbance or increase, any sign that the symbols held the power to open a doorway.

"Uh, guys. Check this out. I'm thinking Ari's doorway works." Crank stood next to the wall with her hand inside. Gone.

Relief washed over me, making my knees weak. We were really doing this. Going into Athena's realm. I sat down and rubbed a shaky hand down my face.

After the shock and reality dimmed, Henri, Sebastian, and I secured our backpacks over our shoulders. I pulled out my τέρας blade with one hand and drew my 9mm with the other. Henri swung a shotgun off his back, which he had strapped there like a bow, and Sebastian went empty-handed. His hands were—as I'd seen—pretty destructive things.

"See you guys soon." I hugged Crank and Dub, and then waited for the others to say good-bye.

Deep breath. Game face on. "Last one in's a rotten egg," I said, and walked through the gate.

Seventeen

I took two steps through the doorway and stumbled, falling forward. My forehead cracked against something hard. A grunt broke from my lips as I dropped to my knees. Shit. That hurt.

It was pitch-black. The smell of earth and water was strong, but cleaner than the musty scent of swamp I was used to. I heard shuffling and breathing to my right. A curse to my left. The guys were through.

"Who the hell put a wall in the way?" Henri groaned.

I slipped my gun back into my waistband and ran my hand over the obstacle in front of me. Grooves, evenly spaced and smooth. "We must be in the ruined temple," I said in a low voice. "This feels like part of a column."

"I think we should keep the flashlights off until we know what's in here," Sebastian said.

"Let's feel our way out of here," I said.

It was slow going, squeezing through spaces, climbing over columns. I'd never been there before, but it sure as hell felt like we were somewhere deep inside the temple. Slowly my eyes adjusted to the darkness, and I could make out shapes that told the story—the temple had partly collapsed; several of the interior columns had fallen and broken apart.

Eventually dim light appeared, illuminating the marble around what I hoped was an exit.

"Thank God," Henri whispered as we approached a small slanted space as wide as a closet door. It had once been a massive doorway, but a large slab of marble had fallen, wedging itself into the space.

The opening was overgrown with vines and roots. It looked like heaven to me, a bright, wonderful, welcoming light.

From darkness to light, I thought, stepping out. *From one world to another.* My eyes adjusted to the soft gray light.

The columns that had collapsed were colossal. I turned and stepped backward to the very edge of a wide landing and craned my neck. The temple still stood, but had buckled, one side slightly collapsed inward, with giant cracks in the marble.

Athena's temple. Well, hers before she stole her father's. And even ruined, it was awe-inspiring.

"Do you guys have any idea how insane this is?" Henri asked, amazed. "This is . . . we're standing in fucking Olympus."

Sebastian let out a low, disbelieving laugh.

I turned away from the temple to see them side by side at the top of the steps, staring out over the landscape. I joined them and the three of us stood, shoulder to shoulder, completely slack-jawed.

Thick woods flanked the temple grounds. To the right was an eerie-looking stone garden, and in front of us, down the steps and beyond the overgrown lawn, was the smooth dark water of a lake.

My gaze traveled over the large expanse of water to the far side of the lake, and past a marble gazebo and a manicured lawn to an enormous white-columned temple that would've given any Ancient Wonder of the World a run for its money.

No doubt in my mind we were gawking at Zeus's temple.

The lake, the land . . . it looked as though it had been plopped down on the side of a jagged mountain. Fires burned from giant bowls around the perimeter of Zeus's temple, and from this distance, I knew they must be the size of swimming pools. Beautiful trees dotted the lawn. A pair of cranes took flight. The faint thrum of a string instrument wafted over the lake.

Heaven. A Maxfield Parrish heaven.

Athena, the goddess of war, destroyer of entire pantheons, and sick narcissistic bitch, lived in a fucking paradise.

For some reason, I'd expected her to live in the hell she seemed to spread in her wake, that she sat on some skulled-out throne and tossed bones to hellhounds. But no. She lived over there. In that beautiful place of horrors.

After the shock wore off, we went down the wide steps. This place was so different from the one across the lake. Vines crawled over everything, snaking up the temple as though trying to pull it down into the earth. It was a dark, lost, and abandoned place, reminding me of the GD.

"Ari, check this out," Henri called from somewhere on the grounds.

I went down the stairs and to my right. The land sloped gently toward a field littered with marble and debris and what looked like hundreds of standing stones. A high wall surrounded the place on three sides.

Lichen, vines, and moss grew over small columns and marble. Stone slabs jutted up at odd angles from the ground. Trees grew around random stones, their roots encasing the hard rock. I saw Henri ahead of me, weaving between the stones.

The fine hairs on my body rose, and a very disturbing sense formed in my gut. Sebastian came to a stop beside me. "What is this place?" I asked in a near whisper.

"You hear that?"

"Hear what?"

"The silence. No birds. No insects. No squirrels climbing up trees. No wildlife here at all."

Maybe that was why I felt so spooked.

Sebastian started off toward Henri. I followed, and once I got a closer look at the stones, an "Oh my God" breezed through my lips and hung there in shock.

They were statues. Hundreds of them. They were old. Random. Eerie. Of warriors, children, women. Some broken forever. Some covered in lichen or swamped in vines, like chains holding them in place.

My heart pounded hard as I picked my way through the stone garden.

I stopped, coming around a statue of a hooded woman in a fall of fabric. Gray marble fabric. Her face was turned to the side, staring as though she'd heard a sound. Vines grew over her sandaled feet and crept up her gown.

Blood rushed past my eardrums. I gulped, reaching out to touch the marble hand that held the cloak closed at her neck. Movement behind me made me stop. I stepped back, away from the statue.

Sebastian threaded his way through Athena's garden of stone. I didn't want to call to him. My voice would be too loud here, too . . . wrong. I crawled over a broken marble bench and hurried to his side. He turned as I approached. His eyes were solemn, his entire being quiet.

This place was like being in church.

Church of the Damned, maybe.

"This is . . . bizarre," he said, looking around.

My chest tightened until it burned. There was no question what this was. "This is more than bizarre. This is a cemetery, Sebastian. Don't ask me how I know it, but these people were turned to stone."

The handiwork of one or maybe hundreds of my ancestors.

"Athena collected these, you think?" Henri approached us. "Pretty morbid, if you ask me."

Tell me about it. "I wonder if she brought the statues here. . . . Or maybe a gorgon actually lived here."

"How can you be sure this is the work of a gorgon?" Henri asked.

We started back toward the temple, passing a marble warrior. A Roman. Young. Handsome. Sword raised. I shivered. "Because I know. . . . It's a feeling. I can't explain it."

I went around a fallen warhorse and found a mother on the other side clutching a toddler to her chest, the child's chubby arm stuck out over a blanket. The mother's face was frozen in fear as though looking in the eyes of Death itself. And the child, the child had its head turned too, looking at me. No fear. It had no idea what it was seeing when it died.

My throat thickened until it was hard to swallow. This was what awaited me. This was what would happen if I refused to end my own life. I'd turn into something that did . . . this, to innocent people.

"Come on. Let's scout a path around the lake. It shouldn't take us long to get to the temple. Twenty, thirty minutes, maybe," Sebastian said, and I was glad for the change in direction.

With the lake butting up to the mountain on one side, our path was chosen for us. We went to the right instead, forging through the woods. The deeper we went, the more thick the vines. They covered the treetops, their long, thin roots hanging down like streamers. If the place had a name, it'd be the Forest of a Thousand Ropes.

After the forest of ropes, the woods became thick and eventually so dense and crowded with undergrowth that I fell behind. Thorns grabbed at my clothes and hands. Branches smacked my face and arms and tangled in my hair. I lost count of how many times I was poked, scratched, or stuck. Or how many curses went through my head or hissed out my mouth.

It was either distract myself or completely lose it. I caught up with Sebastian and tossed out a question that had been brewing ever since my face-to-face meeting with Gabriel and his friends in study hall. "So what's with you and Anne Hawthorne?"

Not one of my smoother moments. More of a jarring, bumbling blurt. I was looking down, watching my step, when Sebastian stopped. I ran straight into his back.

He tossed a curious gaze over his shoulder and kept moving. "Where'd that come from?"

"Uh, from the way she was looking at you. I am a girl. I can tell history when I see it." I shoved a loose wisp of hair from my face with an annoyed swipe.

"We went out a few times."

I waited for more, walking several feet before finally realizing he wasn't going to elaborate. I rolled my eyes and then glared at his back.

"What's your idea of a few times?" I pressed.

He shrugged. "I don't know. It was last year. Didn't work out."

"Why di—" I tripped, recovering before I fell. I groaned in frustration. The urge to pull out my blade and start hacking at the forest was so strong, but I didn't want to dull the blade.

"Look," Henri said in front of us. Random patches of dim firelight from the temple slashed through the thinning woods. "We're getting close. We should go silent from here."

The path began to narrow the closer we got, and I saw sky through the trees to my right where the woods dropped off into nothing. Who knew how far up on the mountain we were—pretty high, if I had to guess.

Finally the woods gave way to a narrow stretch of jagged rocks that curved around to the lawn. The rocks were tall enough that we found cover easily. "Let's stop and rest here," Sebastian suggested.

I slumped to the ground behind a gray rock and dug in my pack for a drink.

"I'm gonna do some aerial recon," Henri announced after a few minutes. "Be back soon."

"Be careful," Sebastian told him. "We don't know what things fly in these skies."

Henri nodded, climbed over the rocks, and then disappeared. I waited, knowing he'd appear in the sky above. Goose bumps spread up my arms as he shot upward like a shadowy dart.

"Pretty cool, right?" Sebastian's head tipped to the sky.

Way cooler than turning into a snake-headed monster, I thought. "If I wasn't afraid of heights, sure. How does he do that, exactly? Where do his clothes go?"

Sebastian laughed, taking a spot across from me and stretching his legs out in front of him. "It's not only a physical thing—otherwise it'd take hours for his body to break down and re-form into a bird. It's magic, Ari," he said with a shrug. "Henri was born into a family of fliers."

"Your father said demigods and shape-shifters are often one and the same."

He drank deeply from his water bottle, his Adam's apple bobbing in a weirdly attractive way. He finished and then swiped a hand across his mouth. "There's probably a god *way* back in Henri's family tree. A lot of shifters have no clue who they're descended from. Over time things get lost or forgotten." He studied me. "Why did you ask me about Anne?"

My heart stuttered, not expecting the change in subject. I unwrapped my granola bar slowly. "I don't know." I took a bite, giving myself time to think through my answer.

This whole boy/girl thing didn't exactly come naturally to me, but I'd seen my share of relationships and the crazy mind games that a lot of people played. "Honestly, if there's something left between you two, I guess I'd rather know up front. I mean, you and I . . . there's no promises or anything, and that's cool, but I'm not into the whole triangle thing, so . . ."

Maybe coyness was *better*, I thought as my face turned hot. At least then I could've avoided feeling like an idiot laying everything on the table like that.

"I'm not into games or playing the field either," he said quietly, eyes thoughtful. "When we make it through this, I want to see where things lead." He cleared his throat. "With you, if you want."

My stomach went weightless. Our gazes stayed locked, and while I answered him in my head, it seemed to take forever to get the words out of my mouth. "I'd like that," I finally managed, breaking eye contact.

When I chanced a second look at him, the corners of his eyes crinkled. I felt a lopsided grin begin to grow and was about to laugh when Henri returned.

He climbed around the rock and went for his bag as he sat on the ground. "The temple is massive." He tipped his head back and drank. "Lots of servants and guards. Seven buildings besides the temple, but none of them look like they're being used as a prison. There's some kind of party going on in the garden. It leads right into the temple, so I say we wait a few hours until everyone is passed out and then we move in for a closer look."

"How's the path from here?" Sebastian asked.

"There's a long wall running from these rocks up the edge of the lawn to the temple. It separates the garden from a drop-off. We're on the side of a mountain. There's nothing but a rocky cliff on the other side of the wall."

I polished off my granola bar and then positioned my backpack to use as a pillow. "Okay, so we wait. Might as well get some rest. From the sound of it, it's going to be a long night."

We settled in to the distant sounds of voices, laughter, and music.

Eighteen

"Time to move." Sebastian nudged me.

I sat up, instantly awake. I'd fallen asleep, which surprised me given the circumstances. My hip and shoulder ached from the hard, rocky bed, and my muscles protested as I stood.

The air was cooler, and the night sky was bright with stars. Everything was quiet, almost peaceful. I slung my bag over my shoulder and made sure my weapons were secure.

We climbed over and around the rocks until we came to the shoreline of the lake. A stone wall rose out of the rocks, trailing up the lawn toward the temple and providing a barrier against the cliff on the other side.

"Stay close to the wall," I whispered as we moved over the grass and passed the white marble gazebo that overlooked the lake.

The sweet fragrance of flowers hung in the air. Cherry and apple trees filled with pink and white blossoms dotted the lawn. A soft breeze sent petals floating through the air like snowflakes.

My heart rate increased the closer we came to the massive temple. Even though it was late, the fires still burned in the pool-size urns.

Zeus's temple rose at least four stories high, maybe five at the peak, and was breathtaking. Colossal. And intimidating as hell. Only the crackling of the large fires split the silence, occasionally sending sparks into the air.

As we neared the long open side of the temple Henri handed his backpack to Sebastian and his shotgun to me. I slung it over my shoulder as he shifted into the hawk and flew to one of the columns to act as lookout.

"It's too quiet," I whispered to Sebastian, my back pressed flat against the stone wall. We were in shadow, but if anyone looked hard enough, they'd spot us. "Don't you think?"

Just as he was about to respond, a couple stumbled drunkenly from the temple and into the garden. They tripped and fell into the grass, laughing. The guy rolled on top of the woman, murmured words into her hair, and then kissed her.

Shit. We wouldn't get by them unnoticed.

I nudged Sebastian, mouthing, *Now what?*

Sebastian straightened his shoulders. His focus zeroed in

on the couple and his jaw clenched. He separated himself from the wall and walked straight out into the open like he belonged there. It took a lot of nerve to do that. I held my breath as he stopped by the couple's shoulders. They looked up as he knelt down. He spoke in a low, friendly, soothing tone. The man spoke back and then resumed kissing his lady. Sebastian continued to the entrance, pressing himself flat against the stone and then ducking his head inside for a look.

He waved me over. I hesitated a second before drawing on my courage and darting out into the open.

I was halfway to Sebastian when an arrow thunked into the ground six inches from my foot. Shock rooted me to the spot. I caught Sebastian's widening gaze and glanced from him to Henri and then to the direction the arrow had originated from.

No, no, no!

For a moment we stayed frozen, so stunned that none of us knew what to do.

Sebastian's eyes took on a feral light. His head turned slowly in the direction of the archer as he let the packs slide off his shoulders. A sudden, oppressive charge filled the air. Could it be from Sebastian? Oh, shit. It had to be, because he looked like a predator about to attack.

I took a step back from the arrow, unsure of what was happening. I'd never felt anything like this from him.

The archer was in the shadows near the corner of the temple. And I knew from her silhouette that it was Menai, the archer who had sat next to me at Athena's table. She'd been so uncaring and nonchalant about my father's torture.

And for that I was going to make her hurt.

I grabbed the grip of my gun as I saw her string another arrow. Henri took flight. The bow lifted and Menai aimed at me. Sebastian charged into my line of sight before I could fire—shit! I released the pressure on the trigger as Henri picked off the arrow before it found a target and flew it out over the wall, releasing it.

Sebastian slammed into Menai. I ran, the backpack and shotgun sliding off my shoulder and to the ground. I leaped over the oblivious couple on the ground. The force of Sebastian's impact sent him and Menai tumbling from the edge of the garden and into the main courtyard at the front of the temple.

Even as I ran, my pulse thundering in my ears, I knew we were screwed. I slid to a stop in the courtyard. Half the space was already ringed with Athena's minions. All the same, all watching the fight, waiting . . .

A tumbling blur shot past me, so fast and so close that my hair moved in the wind. Sebastian and the archer slammed into the wide steps that led into the temple. Marble cracked. They rolled again and she was up, stringing her bow with supernatural speed and firing it before I could even release the scream building in my throat. The arrow sank into Sebastian's shoulder as he leaped to his feet, a ball of blue light already forming in his hands.

The light burst and dissipated as soon as the arrow hit him. He sat down, stunned.

I launched myself at Menai, taking her to the ground. A surprised shriek flew from her as we hit the dirt and rolled. In a flash of inhuman speed she was out from under me, had flipped me over, and was sitting on top of my chest with one of her arrows clenched in her hands, holding it above my jugular. Her hand shook with anger.

I struggled to move, but she wouldn't budge. "No one attacks me. Twice. And lives." She apparently hadn't forgotten about the fork I'd shoved into her hand.

A click sounded. Henri stood in his human form, chest heaving, with his shotgun to her head. "This shotgun shell has about four hundred pellets inside. You might be immortal, but I doubt you'd fully recover from that blasting through your skull."

She came back with what sounded like a string of curses in Greek.

Sebastian hissed in pain, but I couldn't take my eyes off her. "What are you?"

"I am . . ." She struggled with indecision, probably about

whether to try and shove the arrow into my throat or dodge the shotgun. "Faster than you."

"Oh, bravo, Menai!" Athena called from the steps of the massive temple. "You almost had all three of them." Athena swept down the steps looking gorgeous in a flowing white gown and loose hair.

Henri's mouth dropped open.

Menai released me as Athena approached. I rolled to my side and crawled to Sebastian. "Sebastian . . ."

His skin had gone pale and sallow, and blood was already darkening his shirt. His hand gripped the arrow shaft. It trembled. "Need to get this out," he rasped, then clenched his lips into a tight line.

"Here, allow me." Athena stopped on the steps next to us, reached down, and jerked the arrow from his shoulder at a painful angle. Sebastian screamed. Blood bloomed faster over his shirt.

"What do I do? Tell me what to do." I stumbled over my words as Athena sauntered over to Henri, closed his mouth for him with a finger under his chin, grabbed the barrel of his shotgun, flipped it in her hand, and fired it into his stomach.

"Henri!" Oh God. Henri. This wasn't happening. This couldn't be happening.

He grabbed his gut, his expression one of astonished horror, before he crumpled to the ground. Athena motioned for her guards. "Dump him over the cliff."

"NO!"

She spun, holding out a hand to stop me. I was unable to move forward. "You're full of surprises, Aristanae. You must tell me how you made it into my realm. Once you've had some time in my prison."

Nineteen

"I'll heal, Ari," Sebastian muttered as I helped him to his feet. "Warlock vampire, remember? Christ, Henri . . ."

The guards lifted Henri's body, carried him to the wall, and dumped him over. Just like that. As though he was nothing.

I gritted my teeth until tiny bursts of pain shot through my jaw, and I made a promise to Henri—one more person who deserved justice.

My grief became detachment. My shock became determination.

Come hell or high water, Athena was going to pay.

Menai shoved us up the steps to the temple as Athena disappeared inside. I held on to Sebastian's arm tightly, too shocked and sickened to cry. My limbs were trembling so badly, and another push from behind made me trip up the steps. I recovered in time to avoid a face plant on the landing.

At the top of the steps I craned my neck, my gaze going up and up and up. . . . The bases of the columns alone were taller than me. The gods weren't giants as far as I could tell, but their egos—well, one in particular—were definitely in line with the massive structure.

We passed through the main hall, the same room that had held the banquet with my father as the night's entertainment. Fires burned in the stone bowls around the room. But it was empty now and quiet.

After walking the length of a long corridor, we were directed down curved, torch-lit stairs made of stone and into a chamber where several of Athena's τέρας were gathered. At the far end of the chamber we passed through a heavy door and down into the mountain itself, on steps carved into the rock.

A cavernous space opened up two flights down. The steps ended, replaced by a sloping spiral path that ringed a vast chasm. Fall off the ledge and you'd be history. Around the spiral I could make out rooms and prison cells, levels upon levels of them.

Humidity dampened my skin, and the air was thick and difficult to breathe. We proceeded around the chasm, eventually stopping at a row of empty cells. Sebastian and I were put into adjacent cells. The doors slammed shut behind us, the metal clang and lock shuddering through me. The floor was rock and dirt. No bedding, no toilet. The back wall was solid rock and thick bars made up the sides and front.

After Menai and the guards left, I started pacing. "Can you do your disappearing thing?"

"Not right now," he said through a grunt of pain, sitting back against the bars that separated our cells.

I sat down, angled so I could see his face. "I'm sorry." He turned his head toward me. He'd gone even paler than before, a sickly color, and was damp with sweat. "As soon as you're better," I said, "I want you to leave this place, Sebastian. Okay?"

"Leave," he repeated through pants, turning his head away from me and letting it fall back against the bars. His Adam's apple slid up and down as he tried to swallow. "You're crazy. How 'bout when the time comes *you* leave."

I gave a small snort and resisted the urge to tell him that this was *my* fight. He'd made it clear before that he didn't agree with me, and deep down I knew he was right; Sebastian had a legitimate reason to be here too. Yet look where we were. In less than twenty-four hours one of my greatest fears had come true. Athena had struck again, hurting someone I cared about. Two someones. Sebastian was hurt and Henri was . . . gone.

"Ari, it's not working." I saw that his arm was lifted, palm open and trembling. "I can't draw energy here."

He'd expected light to form over his hand and there was nothing. "Can you heal?" I asked.

"Healing is part of my physical makeup, not magic, so yeah. But I can't . . . there must be some kind of spell or block here."

I wasn't surprised. "Your father said the same about the prison Athena kept him in. Maybe it will come back once we get out of here."

"Or she might have her entire temple blocked." He frowned and blinked at me. "She doesn't have you blocked, though."

"What do you mean?"

"What you did to the archer, the last time we were here. You were able to use your power, Ari. Which means"—he stopped to take a few breaths—"she hasn't blocked you in her hall. Maybe here in the prison, but not the hall. She wants to see you use your power. Otherwise she would've killed you already."

And Athena was going to use whatever means possible to see what I was made of. Violet. My father. Sebastian.

"Well, we know magic isn't blocked outside. She won't leave us in here forever. That's not her style." Athena was a showman; she'd make sure all her followers saw exactly what she could do to me and mine. It was obvious that my power was still chaotic and uncontrollable. She knew I was an amateur, and she knew she had the upper hand. My only hope was that she'd let it go to her head, get too comfortable, and make a mistake.

Sebastian's head slumped to the side. "Sebastian?"

He didn't respond. He was out cold.

I grabbed hold of a rusty metal bar and drew my knees to my chest. If I could just think of a plan. . . .

Ideas came and went and nothing seemed viable. Worries and images of what happened in the courtyard kept invading my mind and breaking my concentration. Finally I gave up and closed my eyes. Henri might've made it; he was a shifter and had abilities beyond that of a human. But how could anyone have survived that blast? How could anyone survive being dumped over a cliff?

I rubbed my wet eyes. The hot, tight pain in my chest grew until I could hardly breathe.

Oh God. Henri was dead.

I woke to find myself curled against the wall, my hand through the space in the bars, my fingers entwined with Sebastian's. I didn't know if it was the next day or night. There was no sense of time in the darkness below Athena's temple.

I released Sebastian's hand and sat up, rubbing my face to stir the blood and wake myself up.

Sebastian yawned and straightened, the movement making him wince.

"How's your shoulder?"

He rolled it. "Fine. Just stiff."

I stood and stretched, my stomach growling loudly. My internal clock said it was morning, but there was no way to be sure. No way to eat since our backpacks with our food and water had been confiscated.

On the other side of the wide chasm the cells continued their spiral down into the blackness. One after another, so small from where I stood, so dark and so many. A few sporadic torches burned, but they were too dim and too far away to allow me to see what else occupied the cells.

It wouldn't be long now. Anxiety flooded my system, and I rubbed my arms and paced the cell. Athena would wake and eventually send for us. Which meant I needed to be prepared for anything.

"Ari. Stop."

"I can't help it." I gestured toward the cell door, the sense of helplessness suffocating. "They're going to come, and the next time we go up there, it won't be my father in that pool. . . ."

"Yeah. So stop it."

"If you don't like what I'm feeling, then just block me."

A frown pulled his eyebrows together. "Or just stop projecting. You think I *want* to feel what you're feeling right now? You think I liked feeling what you felt when you saw your father? I don't. I don't. . . ." He dropped his head in his hands, rubbed his face, and then plowed his fingers through his hair.

I knelt down in front of him, grabbed the bars, and shook my head. "I don't know what to do."

He reached through and lifted a strand of my hair, twisting it around his hand. "You're not responsible for all this, you know. And it won't be your fault if we fail. It's not your fault that Henri is gone. . . ."

I stared down at the floor, suddenly finding it very interesting. That was the heart of it, wasn't it? If we did fail, if Sebastian or Violet got hurt or worse during all this, I'd blame myself. I'd see it as my fault, that I should've saved them, done something differently. . . .

My nose grew stuffy. I lost myself for a minute in the storm clouds in Sebastian's eyes. He tugged on my hair. "You're doing it right now, aren't you? That calming thing."

"No." He shrugged. I laughed sadly, then sniffed again.

Keys jingled in the lock. The guards had returned. Desperation blew cold and bitter through me. I wasn't ready for this. I shook my head, looking at Sebastian. His fingers wrapped around mine on the bars. We didn't move until they came inside each of our cells and pulled us apart.

We were taken to the main hall in the temple. Music played, but this time it was David Bowie's "China Girl," which at first surprised me, but then I remembered what I'd learned about

Athena involving herself in every era of civilization. Guess she liked Bowie.

I spotted Menai sitting on a bench, sharpening the tips of her arrows. Groups of Athena's minions gambled and drank and messed with the female servants.

The tables were being set for another feast.

Menai saw us, got up, and approached. She grabbed Sebastian and snapped a gold cuff around his wrist. "The only way you can get this off is if you remove your hand, so don't waste your time."

The cuff was three inches wide and ringed with symbols.

"What's it for?" I noticed she didn't have one for me.

"Athena wants to see you in the garden. This will prevent him from using magic outside the temple. You she doesn't see as a threat." She smirked at me and gestured for the guards to continue.

I knew Athena wanted me to use my power, but I had to wonder if she would be able to block me in the first place. Unlike Sebastian, I didn't draw on energy. I didn't use magic. My power came from Athena's words, her curse. Maybe she had no spell or jewelry for that. Or maybe she was just messing with my head.

Beyond the long line of tables were columns that led into the garden, walled on two sides. The sun had just set, leaving the sky a mix of purple, pink, and fading orange. Apparently, my inner clock was way off. A breeze blew over the garden. I drew the clean, fragrant air into my lungs—so welcome after the thick heat of the prison.

Several cherry trees in full bloom dotted the garden. White and pink blossoms floated in the air, landing on my hair and shoulders. Ahead of us columns rose up to form a rectangular gazebo, and beyond it was the lake.

My boots sank into the soft grass. We walked up the three wide steps into the marble gazebo set with chaise lounges, chairs, and tables.

The sound of a splash drew my attention. The guards released us and stepped back to hover just outside the structure. I walked to the other side of the gazebo, staring down the gentle slope of grass dotted with tall trees to the banks of the water.

Athena was walking from the water, hair slicked back and wet, her black one-piece bathing suit glistening. She held a small white alligator cradled in one arm; it practically glowed against the black of her suit. Pascal. Without a doubt, I knew it was him. Athena bent down and let him crawl off her forearm onto the gray rocks.

My breath hitched as he waddled over the rocks toward a small child sitting with her back propped against a rock. I couldn't see her face, but the tiny pale hands that reached out and gathered the alligator into her lap were unmistakable.

"It's Violet," I breathed, goose bumps shooting up my arms and thighs.

No wonder I hadn't found Pascal; he was here with Violet. Athena must have sent one of her minions to get him and bring him here. She was trying to win Violet over even though the little girl had stabbed her in the heart. The question was, why?

"Don't turn your head, but look up to your right," Sebastian said quietly.

A hawk was perched high in a tree overlooking the lake. Second shock of the day. I had to force myself not to gape. "Do you think . . . ?"

"I don't know. Let's pray like hell it is."

If Henri had survived . . . Hope stirred in my chest, but it was a tight, hot feeling, one that was too afraid to believe such a thing was possible.

Athena had approached Violet and was speaking to her in soft, friendly tones, and then she looked up and saw us. She spoke to Violet again, and then Violet vanished, simply gone.

Athena sauntered up the grassy hill. In midstep she went from bathing suit to white Greek gown. The kind you see on ancient statues. Her hair was piled onto her head and set with a simple gold band. The material of the gown brushed the tips of gold sandals. She finally looked the part of Greek goddess.

She lifted the gown and came up the steps, letting it fall once she reached the floor of the gazebo. "Enjoying your stay?" She swept past us, motioning to the guards to bring us along.

We had no choice but to follow her back through the garden. The fires around the temple had been lit, and it was nearly dark now. The light from the temple's interior glowed brightly. The noise and smells of another feast drifted in the air.

Inside, food and drink were being set onto the tables and guests had already been seated. My blood pressure rose. I knew I couldn't handle watching my father ripped to shreds again.

When I saw that the pool had been covered with a slab of thick wood, I almost sank to my knees in relief. Then one of the guards yanked Sebastian away from me and my heart dropped like a stone. My guard took me to Athena's table and shoved me into a chair next to her as Sebastian was led to the covered pool.

The wooden slab was polished and smooth. Bolted into the wood were metal rings. The guards forced Sebastian onto the platform and then to his knees. They chained him to the rings. Once they were done, they left him, ankles and wrists shackled with enough slack for him to move, but not enough to stand.

My throat went dry and thick as dread-laced panic began to gather, pushing my heart rate into overdrive.

Athena dropped down beside me. "I bet you're dying to know what I plan. It's going to be good, a stroke of genius, really." She gave me a smug look and then nodded to her left.

A woman stepped from the shadows. The firelight passed through the sheer material of her gown, outlining the shape of her hips and breasts. Her dark hair was down, falling in waves to her lower back.

She walked toward Sebastian like they were the only ones in existence. The males in the room followed her with lust in their eyes as she circled around the platform and then stopped behind Sebastian.

His eyes found mine and locked on.

Time stopped.

She stepped onto the wood, went down on her knees behind him, and pressed her front against his back, trailing her hands over his arms and finally tilting his head to one side. Exposing his neck.

And then with sickening clarity, I understood.

Athena leaned close to me, her shoulder brushing mine. "Zaria is one of the most gluttonous vampires I've ever known. She particularly loves to drink from other vampires."

Sebastian's gaze never wavered. He seemed to separate himself from what was happening by latching on to me. I couldn't look away, *wouldn't* look away, not when he needed me.

I sat there, nails digging into my palms and tears blurring my vision. I had power and I was such an amateur loser that I couldn't control it, couldn't even concentrate enough to stir anything.

Athena patted my arm. "It's okay, little gorgon. You're just a baby. No one expects you to save him. Not that he'll want to be saved." She chuckled.

The hate that gripped me was harsher and more vicious than anything I'd ever known. And it stirred the monster in me. My eyelids slid closed and I directed my concentration deep within me.

"Chill, gorgon," Athena hissed in my ear, "or you'll miss the best part."

I shouldn't have looked. Looking made me lose the tiny hold I'd gained over my power.

From behind, Zaria looped one arm around Sebastian's chest and the other over his forehead, holding his head back at an angle against her. And then she sank her fangs into his neck.

A moan filled the room. Her moan. A trickle of blood ran down Sebastian's pale skin. His eyes blinked once with her pierce and then they stayed on me.

My heart hammered so fast, I went dizzy, swaying in my seat and having to grab the table for support.

The beings in the room watched in fascination, some eating slowly as the vampire went on drinking for what seemed like an eternity.

I couldn't eat, couldn't do anything but watch. When she lifted her head, her lips were ringed in red and her eyes glowed.

The light in Sebastian's eyes dimmed and they dropped from me.

He was as white as the marble outside. I started to weep.

Zaria's knees gave out and she sat, pulling Sebastian down with her, cradling him in her lap. He looked up at her. She kissed him softly before motioning to another woman standing nearby—a servant, from the looks of her clothing, and one who appeared to be under Zaria's spell. The servant stepped onto the platform, sank to her knees, and held out her wrist. Zaria dragged her fingernail across the servant's skin. Blood flowed against pale skin.

Zaria took the woman's wrist and held it to Sebastian's nose, urging him to taste, letting the blood flow over her arms and down the side of his chin to soak his shirt.

The woman must be human, her blood more enticing. . . .

Sebastian trembled; even from this distance I could see it. The chains rattled. My body had turned to steel, every muscle twisted so tight. I willed him to resist.

But I knew the urge was there. He'd told me it was, lurking in every vampire, whether Bloodborn, Dayborn, or like him, Mistborn.

That need was being drawn out of him whether he wanted it or not.

Athena was forcing him to do something he never wanted to do, something that once he did, he could never change. He never wanted to be an Arnaud, never wanted to be a vampire like his mother's side of the family.

I held my breath, along with what felt like the entire assembly, as he grabbed the woman's wrist. His eyes shone brightly, his face a mask of pain. She winced. And then he shoved her arm aside, refusing to take what she offered, and collapsed against Zaria.

TWENTY

FOR THE NEXT TWO NIGHTS I WATCHED ZARIA AND HER SERVANT tempt Sebastian.

Every night we were returned to our cells and he slumped against the far wall, breathing heavily and nearly completely drained of blood. He wouldn't speak to me, wouldn't get near me. He was starved for food and blood, so weak he was losing his hold on reality.

I was growing weaker as well. Athena piled her plate high every night, yet she only allowed me one cup of water and a chunk of bread. I struggled between sickness and horror as I bore witness to Sebastian's unique form of torture.

I hadn't been able to stir my power again, and I knew it was because I was too weak and my emotions had dulled. I hadn't been touched, otherwise. Athena's brand of torture for me was all mental, all designed—as Bran had said—to mess with me from the inside out.

And Henri—if that had really been Henri out there—had yet to show himself. I had no idea what was happening outside the temple, but I knew Sebastian couldn't hold out forever.

At the end of the third night the guards had to carry Sebastian back to the cell because he was too weak to walk. They dropped him on the floor of his cell, but this time they shoved me inside with him, locking the door behind us.

Sebastian lifted his head, saw me, and screamed, lunging on his knees with renewed strength, grabbing on to the bars. "NO! GET BACK HERE! GET HER OUT OF HERE!"

They walked away laughing.

I went to him, but his hand shot out. "Stay away from me!" he snarled at me, eyes wild and unfocused. I froze. "Get back against the wall, Ari. Don't touch me. Please, don't touch me."

He released the bars and sank to his hands and knees, his head hanging low. He shook all over, his back rising and falling with heavy breathing.

I wrapped my arms around my body, stepping back. "You can't hold out forever," I said, crying. "You're going to die, Sebastian. You can't survive like this." I drew in a deep breath and plowed on. "Just take my blood and get it over with."

His head whipped around, his expression dangerous. "Don't." His low growl gave me goose bumps.

Frustration and desperation kept me talking, rambling on quickly despite his warning. "You'll be stronger, right? If you drink blood, if you become . . ." I couldn't even say the word.

"Shut up, Ari."

"No. I won't shut up. I can't. Athena is going to take this to the very end. One more night and you'll . . . I'm offering to help. You want to die here, like this? On her terms? Just take it."

He swung around, seething with anger and hunger. "I DON'T WANT IT!" He turned away, slumping against the bars. "I'd rather die."

I opened my mouth but then stopped. I couldn't even go and comfort him. "Don't do this," I begged. "Don't make me watch you die when I can save you."

"And give Athena what she wants," he said, his face hidden by his arm.

"If it means you live, then yes."

"I don't want to talk about it anymore. I don't want it. I don't want *you*. Leave me alone."

I moved away from him until my back hit the rock wall. I slid down, pulling my knees to my chest, hugging them, and staring at the form curled against the bars.

Sebastian held on to those bars as though they'd save him.

But they wouldn't; the only thing that could save him was me. And we both knew it. Athena had designed this little bit of torture very carefully. The hunger and psychological crap she put him through night after night had taken him to his breaking point.

Here in her realm Sebastian had no powers, and while he could heal faster than a human, he wasn't immortal yet. She'd backed me into a corner. There was no way I could sit there and watch him die. One more night was all it would take . . . if he lived through this one.

I rested my chin on my knees as my thoughts churned. After a while Sebastian's grip on the bars eased, and his posture slumped as he yielded to sleep—or unconsciousness; it was hard to tell.

I bit softly on the inside of my cheek, exhausted but too freaked out to close my eyes and rest. Athena was definitely living up to her reputation as the most cunning strategist around. Goddess or not, though, she had to have a weakness. And if it wasn't power and control, then maybe her weakness lay in her personal life. After all, that's where she was hitting me the hardest, so why not turn the tables?

But Athena's personal life and those she loved were a mystery to me—if she even loved; that emotion and ability might've been lost a long time ago. Which would explain a lot.

My eyelids finally became heavy, and weariness muddled my thoughts. I rubbed both dirty hands down my damp face, smearing the old tears away. Why was I even trying to come up with a way to beat her? I was a seventeen-year-old peon compared to her, a mouse facing a *T. rex*.

Waves of hopelessness crashed down on me. My ability to think and reason fled, leaving only a fierce pain in my gut that hurt the most in quiet times when everything else faded away and the distractions of emotions dulled. But even that eventually gave way to sleep.

I woke hot and feverish, unsure of how long I'd been out. My rear hurt and my back had gone painfully stiff. I saw legs in my line of sight. Groggy and confused, I lifted my head. Sebastian stood over me, like a ghost in the dark with his pale skin and bright gray eyes. When our eyes met, he turned away and went back to the bars.

I went in and out of consciousness, my dreams vivid and disturbing, the floor hard and my hunger sharp. Rest was a joke—an annoying, irritating joke.

When I came to again, I was still on my side, arm curled beneath my head. Sebastian sat in the corner awake. I stared at him as my mind cleared and it dawned on me what he was doing.

I sat straight up.

He was hunched over with a sharp rock in his hand, making slice after slice on the soft, pale skin of his forearm, his hand in a tight fist.

Using pain to focus.

Bitter cold shot through my chest. I knew what that was like. "Stop it," I whispered, pushing myself up. My legs shook with weakness. I held on to the wall behind me for support and shoved my hair from my eyes with my other hand.

He didn't stop, didn't even hear me. He was in his own little world.

"Sebastian," I said louder. "Stop it."

Nothing. Over and over he drew thin red lines across his arm.

"Sebastian." I crossed the cell, bent down, and grabbed the rock out of his hand.

The second my skin brushed his, his hand shot out and wrapped tightly around my wrist. Pain tore through my joint as bones and tendons crunched together. I pulled back with a cry, but he held on.

He lifted his head and pierced me with strange silvery eyes set in a face that was somehow more angular, starker, and more frightening than I expected.

In a blur he was up. A gasp lodged in my throat as he grabbed my upper arms and shoved me against the back wall of the cell.

I slammed against the rock, the breath knocked out of me. He pinned me, completely covering my body with his.

I couldn't move and I fought to remain calm, to help him in whatever way I could. His forehead touched the rock wall by my head. His chest rose and fell, and his heart beat so strongly I felt it pounding against my chest like a drum.

Rocks rained onto the floor, and I knew he was digging his nails into the wall, trying to remain in control.

Several seconds passed before I found my voice. "Sebas—"

"Don't talk."

In the quiet, this close to him, every sense stirred and every nerve ending lit with fear and anticipation.

I knew this was it. This was the moment, and . . . I wanted it to be me. Despite Athena bringing us to this point, despite the fact that he didn't want this, I wanted it to be me.

I wanted to be the one to save him.

I drew in a deep breath, forcing myself to relax and accept the inevitable. I still had the rock in my hand, so I moved my free hand to his lower back where his shirt met his jeans, where my palm landed on bare skin.

He shuddered.

His hand slid from the wall, over my head, and down to my temple. "Please stop," he begged me in a gruff, broken tone.

So much pain in his voice. A tear slipped from the corner

of my eye. Bittersweet emotions settled heavy on my heart. He didn't want this.

Athena had known it would come down to this, had made sure it would come down to this. Another tear slipped out. The choice was never his. It was mine. It had always been mine.

His hands delved into my hair, his lips skimming my temple, then down toward my ear. "Stop, Ari. Stop hurting for me. I can't take it. . . ."

His words only made it worse. I started trembling. His thumb trailed over my cheek, hitting the tears. He lifted his head a fraction and kissed my tears away.

Then his wet lips settled on mine.

He stayed there for a long, torturous moment, holding my face still, trying to control himself, his closed lips pressed hard against mine. Shivers raced down my limbs, turning my legs to jelly. Warmth and pleasure mingled with heartbreak as he pressed against me, acting on pure physical instinct.

"I can't." He tore his lips from mine. He was shaking so hard, trying so hard to fight what in the end he simply couldn't.

I knew what I had to do to end his suffering. I lifted the rock in my hand and dragged it hard across my neck. The sting brought a gasp to my lips as my skin split open.

He drew back.

Our eyes met. His nostrils flared; he could smell it, the blood.

Lines in his brow knitted together in need and despair. But it was just a brief, heartrending flash before his eyes went intense and silvery.

I lifted my hand and slipped it around his neck, twining my fingers in his hair and tugging him down.

As his mouth found my neck, I sobbed, "I'm sorry."

His breath feathered across my skin. And then his warm mouth settled on my wound. His tongue swirled out and licked the blood. His body went tight. He pressed me harder against the rock. His mouth opened wider. His teeth grazed my skin.

Then he bit. Hard.

An instant gasp burst from my mouth. The rock dropped from my hand. My nails dug into his sides, but he didn't seem to notice. His heart hammered against mine even faster than before.

The sharp sting slowly receded. As if he sensed it, the decrease in my pain, a moan came from deep within his throat. He sucked harder, that tug shooting all the way to my belly and turning the hurt into a weird kind of pleasure. My eyelids slid closed and my fingers tangled in his hair.

I was lost. No longer cared what happened to me. One of my legs came up to wrap around him, to pull him even closer. His hands slid around my bottom, and he lifted me up, pinning me against the rock wall, holding me there.

Both of my arms wrapped around his neck, and I drifted into a world of warmth and lust.

Eventually my heart rate slowed.

And my world went black.

Twenty-One

I woke with a throbbing headache. My mouth was dry and pasty, and my stomach had curled into a tight, sour knot. I blinked, cracking my hot eyes open, wincing at the low torch-light far down the ledge. Too bright. I pushed myself up slowly and scooted back until I could lean against the wall. The effort had me panting and breaking out in a cold sweat.

I stayed there for several minutes, head back against the wall, eyes closed, and trying not to dry heave or pass out. I hadn't expected this kind of aftereffect. Sebastian must have drunk too much, leaving me with some kind of blood-loss hangover.

My neck throbbed. I turned my head a tiny bit, enough to see that Sebastian was gone. The sounds of footsteps were amplified a million times, and I cringed at the clang of keys in the metal lock. I didn't get up or move. I couldn't. A hand gripped my arm. I raised my middle finger and laughed: a dry, raspy, abrupt sound. Another hand grabbed me, and I was hauled up by my armpits and dragged out of the cell. My head fell forward, dirty hair falling around my face, and my stomach rolled.

Jesus.

Blackness began to bleed into my mind and I let out a grateful sigh before passing out.

I woke to the smell of fresh air and grass. Ah, the garden. The guards released me and I fell forward, sinking into the soft ground and turning my head to rest on the spring-scented pillow. *So nice.*

I lay still, flat out and immersed in goodness. After the heat and hardness of the prison, this was heaven. My hand curled into the grass as a cherry blossom landed on my dirty skin. I grabbed it between two fingers and brought it slowly to my nose, breathing in deeply, about to close my eyes when the sound of laughter and the random melody of a guitar made me hesitate.

I didn't lift my head, just looked at everything from my prone position, processing the flowering trees, the grass, the wall, the bird that sat perched there with his wings folded back, his head cocked as it studied me.

Henri. The hope that ballooned in my chest actually hurt. I

went to rub my eyes to get a better look at the bird, but voices drew my attention to the white marble gazebo.

There were figures there, relaxing, draped over the lounges. Athena's laughter rang out over the garden. A deeper voice followed. I frowned, concentrating hard on the sideways picture until it became crystal clear.

Athena was reclining on one of the chaise lounges, propped on her elbow, her head resting on the palm of her hand. Her feet curled under her.

Sebastian sat on the end of her lounge, plucking at the strings of a guitar. He said something over his shoulder to her and she laughed again. His black hair fell over his brow. He wore a clean white shirt open at the collar and dark pants, and his feet were bare.

The vampire Zaria, who had drunk him repeatedly to the brink of death, reclined on the other lounge. The woman whose wrist Zaria had cut sat on the floor while Zaria played with the woman's hair.

Trying to process the scene was like trying to convince myself that the tooth fairy existed; it just didn't compute. This was a dream, a lie, a reality that could never, ever be. . . .

I didn't care what I was seeing. It wasn't fucking real.

My heart knocked hard against my rib cage. Why was he there? Why was he with them?

I pushed my stiff, weak body up to a sitting position. I weaved back and forth, setting my hands in the grass to stop myself from falling. I stayed like that until my balance returned and the dizziness passed. Then I crawled inch by inch to the garden's fountain.

The dribbling water sounded so lovely and bizarre and ridiculous. The marble was cold, wonderfully cold. I pulled myself up, balancing my chest on the rim of the fountain, and dipped my hands into the clean water. My lips were cracked, and the liquid felt so good on them that I let out a sigh.

I drank greedily; that first hit of cold water sent spasms of pain through my empty stomach, but I kept on drinking.

After I'd had enough, I splashed the water on my dry, dirty face and then patted some onto the bite mark on my neck. The pulsating heat ebbed. God, it felt so good.

Feeling stronger, I pushed the rest of the way onto the wide rim of the fountain and sat down. It was difficult to keep my head up since it felt as heavy as a bowling ball.

A breeze went through the garden, the gentle current carrying white blossoms from the trees. They swirled around me, falling on my knees and hands, floating on the water in the fountain. I stared at the petals on my hand. So pretty and clean and fragrant.

Unlike me. Unlike the cell. Unlike last night—or whenever

the hell it was—which had been raw and intense. And life-changing for Sebastian.

Offering him my blood when I knew he'd rather die than become a blood-drinker for the rest of his life . . . I wasn't sure how to feel about it now. I'd done it because I didn't want him to die, couldn't let him throw his life away. I'd done it because he was starving and not thinking straight.

I'd taken the decision away from him.

I'd thought it was the right decision, thought I was saving his life. But now I didn't know what to think.

I don't want it, he'd said. *I'd rather die.*

Damn it. I put my head in my hands. What had he expected? I'd done the only thing I could. And if anything, I had to stand by that decision. I'd make it again if I had to.

With a fortifying breath I finally looked toward the gazebo, no longer able to ignore the music and the soft voices, no longer able to tell myself it wasn't real.

The scene hadn't changed. And my emotions fell like dominoes.

Sebastian was a true Arnaud. Like his mother. Like Josephine.

Why was he there, hanging with Athena and her vampire BFF, playing languid tunes on a twelve-string guitar?

He hadn't cracked a smile or laughed the entire time I watched, but it didn't matter. I didn't want to hear his music or their giggles.

As I withdrew my gaze it snagged on Athena. She was smiling at me.

The arrogance and triumph in her look shattered my soul. She made a smug little wave with her fingers, drawing Sebastian's attention. His head shifted slowly in my direction. My breath held. His gaze went right through me. As though I didn't exist. There was no flicker of . . . anything.

He went back to playing.

A long exhale blew from my lips, ending with a painful sob. I stood, took four retreating steps, and my legs gave out. The bastard had nearly drunk me dry and now he acted like I was a ghost.

I rolled onto my back, the crook of my arm resting against my forehead. Athena came into focus. She stood at my feet, looking down at me with a pleased expression. "He's mine now," she practically purred.

I started laughing. "Grow up, Athena. Or get a therapist. Maybe there's a psychotic bitches support group you could join."

She knelt down, arms draped over her knees. "Oh, I do like the challenge of you, Aristanae. You know, you might be able to kill me one day. But of course, I can do the same to you now, and trust me, I'm better at it. Perhaps by the time you are a real threat, I will have broken you." She shrugged, toying with a blade of grass. "Or you will be dead. We'll see. Until then I will take everyone you love, everyone you care about, and I will make them mine. Not because I want them, but because you do."

She strolled away. I let my head fall to the side and watched as her feet and the hem of her gown drifted across the grass, the blades springing upright in her wake.

I laughed again, pressing my palms against my eyes as the sound turned to sobs.

The guards came at some point and took me down into the heat, the dirt, and the disgusting scent of my cell. Whatever. I lay on the hard ground and stayed there, letting the grief and despair and numbness consume me completely.

I had no idea how many days I spent there. No water, no food, just lying on the floor lost while somewhere above me Athena played with Violet and Sebastian.

I didn't want to think about it, didn't want to imagine them together in my mind, but they crept into my dreams anyway—eating together, strolling in the garden, laughing. . . .

I'd saved his life. I'd given him my blood. And he'd deserted me, walked away from me. Hated me, most likely.

And Athena, she'd written me off, left me in the cell to die. I wasn't immortal. Maybe she'd forgotten that, maybe she no longer cared about breaking me. I chuckled at that. What was I thinking? She already had.

Stupid Ari.

I dreamt of crazy things. My mother and father living in Memphis with me. The eels slithering and twisting around each other, their double jaws snapping. Lafayette Swamp Cemetery growing to cover all of New 2. Visions of Mardi Gras and the gowns and the music and the parades. The eerie stone garden.

When I did wake up, I hallucinated. I saw things—Sebastian in my cell; Violet dancing through the air in her Mardi Gras mask and purple skirt, dancing with Pascal; an alligator man dressed in a tuxedo. Milky snakes slithered on the ground of my cell, striking me in the face and neck, their tiny noses tunneling into my ears and up my nose, trying to force their way into my mouth.

I was dying; in those brief moments of lucidity, I knew it.

I saw Menai, the archer, come into my cell, her flawless face gazing down at me with impatience. I wanted to turn her into a fat cherub whose aim was so bad it'd be a miracle if she managed to hit the ass end of an elephant.

Bubbles of demented laughter rattled my chest.

Yep, that was me. Ari the Mad. Maybe my tombstone would read: THE GORGON WHO LOST HER MARBLES IN A REALM THAT SHOULDN'T EXIST.

"What the hell is she so happy about?" Menai's annoyed tone echoed from far away.

"It is not happiness, I can assure you," came a male voice.

A cloaked figure knelt down and placed a rough hand on my brow. He spoke in a low, urgent voice, deep and resonant. Greek. It was nice, that voice.

Death. Death had come for me. I laughed again. Figures.

"Oh, child," the dark angel whispered in pity. "Menai, pick her up."

Menai gathered me up and slung me over her shoulder. Blood rushed to my head. *Maybe this isn't a hallucination after all,* I thought just before I tumbled gratefully into oblivion.

Twenty-Two

Shadows flickered on the marble wall. Through slits in my eyelids, I traced the shadows back to their source and found fires burning in basins around the outer edges of the tiled floor.

I didn't realize I was lying on the floor naked until water hit me in the face and chest.

I sat up sputtering and choking, chest and lungs straining as water leaked down the wrong pipes. My eyes widened as I tried to get a grip on where I was and what was happening.

Menai stood over me with a bucket. A servant handed her another. She threw the water at me before I could react. It hit me square in the face.

I shrieked and choked again.

After I recovered—somewhat—I began to process my current situation through the pain of a vicious headache. I hadn't been hallucinating. Menai and the cloaked angel had been in my cell and had dumped me in some sort of bath chamber. Nearby, steam rose from a rectangular pool ringed with columns.

I swiped a hand down my face and glared at Menai. "You didn't have very many friends growing up, did you?" It hurt to talk, but I forced the words out anyway.

She snickered. "Probably as many as you." She reached for another bucket. "Stand up."

The scent of my own filth made my gut curl. I was a living, breathing biohazard. I'd been left in that dirty cell for days with no real bathroom except for a hole in a dark corner, no way to clean myself, and no will to do anything about it.

I pushed to my feet, more interested in being clean than being modest. "How is it I can stand?" I straightened, glancing down and seeing my ribs and hip bones jutting out more prominently than before.

"The healer was able to help you some. You are beyond disgusting, by the way." She hit me with more water.

No argument there. I rubbed my skin as dark, dirty water rolled off me and down a drain near my feet. She dumped a few more buckets over my head.

"There. Now you won't pollute the bath." She set the bucket

down. “There’s soap and shampoo. The rest is all you.”

I walked to the steaming bath. A set of steps led into the water. Hot water closed over one foot, then the other. Inch by inch I went in, the raw places on my skin stinging painfully, but I continued until I was neck deep. A tray of soaps, shampoos, and sponges had been placed near the edge of the bath.

Menai sat on a bench along the wall, crossed one ankle over the other, and began picking at her nails. Apparently she was going to be here for the duration. The “healer” was nowhere to be seen.

“Where is the healer? Was he the man in my cell? Who is he?” I selected a bottle of shampoo and then poured as much as I could hold into my palm.

“None of your damn business.”

“Okay. Why was I taken out of the cell, then?”

“Tonight is the Procession. You’re to take part.”

“What’s the Procession?”

She rolled her eyes like I was an idiot. “Every four years since ancient times there’s a festival to honor Athena. It’s called the Panathenaic Procession. It used to be held over several days, but now it’s just one night where the gods come and pay homage to her. They banquet and then sacrifice or torture any enemies caught. . . . That sort of thing.”

Oh, right. That sort of thing.

I scrubbed at my scalp and then pulled my hair over my shoulder to work the shampoo through the strands. The suds were brown. I ducked under to rinse and then added more shampoo to my hair.

"So how many gods come to the Procession?"

"A handful. Mostly relatives—the ones she hasn't killed. If they don't come, she thinks they're plotting against her."

"Makes life easier if they show up," I surmised.

"Something like that, yes."

I ducked under the water to rinse my hair. One more wash should get it clean. I grabbed the shampoo bottle and squeezed more into my palm. "What's my role in the Procession, do you know?" I knew I'd been brought here to get all spiffy for a reason—not a good one, either.

Menai shrugged. "Don't know. Don't care."

"Menai," I said, then paused to think over my words. I knew the whole smart-ass, not-my-problem routine; used it myself on plenty of occasions. *Takes one to know one,* I thought. "Why are you part of all this? You're not like her; you're not evil. You could've shot Sebastian through the heart and yet you didn't."

"Maybe I missed."

"Yeah. I doubt that." Menai didn't strike me as someone who missed. Ever.

A brief look of vulnerability passed over her features, gone before I could even wonder what it meant. "It doesn't matter. Only that Athena controls me and everyone else."

"And my father, have you seen him?"

She gave me a weird look.

My heart dropped. "He's not—"

"No, no," she said quickly. "He's alive and healing. Athena hasn't brought him back out again for the nightly entertainment." Her voice went uncomfortable and then nonchalant. "She's been too busy playing with your strange little friend and your boyfriend." Menai tilted her head, eyes narrowing. "He makes a yummy-looking vampire. I can see why you're into him."

I glared at her; a couple spontaneous kisses and some handholding didn't exactly make Sebastian my boyfriend. It didn't even qualify as a relationship at all; we never even got far. . . .

"My father," I said, drawing her back to whatever the hell it was she *wasn't* saying.

I continued washing as her jaw went tight and her expression turned annoyed once again. Her sharp gaze scanned the room, waiting until a servant walked out of hearing range. "You really don't remember?"

"Remember what?"

Her lips turned down into a frown, and she gave me a very exaggerated *duh* without words.

My hands slowed, eventually stopping completely. "That was

him. In the cell. My father." He came to see me. My father. He spoke. Nice words, whatever they were. Caring words. My throat grew thick. "How?"

"Stay here long enough and guards get paid off, deals get made. We have our own little system in Athena's underground. . . ."

"He healed me, didn't he?" Wow. "He can do that?"

"Uh, yeah. He gave what little he had." Her eyes narrowed in a calculating manner. "Theron's a hunter. He can do lots of interesting—"

The servant came back carrying a heavy basket and then motioned for me to finish in the bath. I got out, dried off, and took the underclothes from the servant, my mind preoccupied with thoughts of my father.

Several sharp tugs around my ribs brought me back to the present as some kind of bustier/breastplate was being laced up like a corset at my back. Next I shimmied into black leather pants. They were slashed in places, on purpose or in battle, I didn't know. Boots were laced to just below my knees—comfy and not high heels, thank God. At least I could run and fight in them.

They attached a black choker around my neck and then began brushing out my clean hair. It had been so dirty from lying day after day on the floor of the cell that I'd forgotten how white it truly was.

I knew Athena was going to have me fight, and all I could

picture was some kind of gladiator-type event, what kind of opponents I'd face, and how I'd beat them, using whatever weapon I'd be given—if any.

My stomach growled and I was allowed bread, fruit, and a small block of cheese to eat as they brushed my hair. My father had worked a miracle on my weakened body; I felt stronger and hungrier, almost normal again.

After all this time jailed, unable to act and having to watch while Athena tortured those I cared for . . . now my time had come. I'd face whatever she threw at me. If she wanted a show, I'd sure as hell give her one.

One of the servants stood in front of me with a sponge and wiped at the small crescent moon tattoo on my cheekbone. I jerked away. "It doesn't come off."

She tried again and I swatted at her hand. She huffed and spoke to me in Greek. I shot a glower at Menai, who was still enamored with her nails. "Will you tell her it won't come off?"

Menai returned my irritated expression. She said a few words, and the servant bowed her head and went to another task—helping to twist the sides of my hair into two long braids, so that they framed my face and kept my hair from falling into my eyes. They left the rest of it long, which sucked because long hair in a fight was a major liability.

"Can you get them to tie my hair back?" I asked Menai.

She rolled her eyes and repeated my request. They shook their heads. Menai shrugged. "Sorry. Not their decision."

Great.

Once they were done, they stepped back and surveyed their handiwork, gesturing and talking among themselves. I guessed they had finally decided I was as good as I was gonna get and left me to Menai.

As soon as they were gone, I took the opportunity to twist my hair and knot it.

Menai strolled over. Her once-over said she wasn't impressed with my new look. "Come on."

I grabbed her arm before she could get beyond my reach. She whirled on me, glanced down at my hand on her arm and then back up at me with a quirk to her eyebrow that said: *Do you really want to go there?*

I didn't let go. "You could fight her or leave."

She jerked out of my grasp. "No. Actually, I can't." She marched away.

I caught up and fell in step beside her. With Menai's dangerous bow, sharp arrows, and supernatural speed, we might be a force to be reckoned with.

Menai was like me. Different. A fighter too. And she wasn't a cold-blooded killer like Athena. Menai didn't belong here. And I desperately needed an ally.

We emerged from the building opposite Athena's temple and headed across the massive courtyard. I thought I'd been in the main temple and had no memory of being taken to a different location.

Servants bustled from one building to another, looking flustered.

"Why don't the other gods fight her?" I asked under my breath as we hurried across the space. "She's letting them into her realm and she doesn't have the Aegis. If they fought together, they could win."

"No, they can't, Ari. She's the goddess of strategy for a reason; she holds something over all of them. They wouldn't dare risk it."

I gritted my teeth. I was tired of hearing how powerful Athena was, how she had everyone wrapped around her finger. No one person could have that much control over everyone and no one person should.

Ancient-sounding music came from the temple—strings and drums and flutes. Several loud cheers echoed from inside. I paused at the steps, my gaze following the tall columns up and up and up.

Menai stopped on the steps. "Gorgon, hurry up."

"It's *Ari*," I said tightly.

"Whatever. Just pick up the pace."

I drew in a deep breath, trying to mentally prepare as I went up the steps and into Athena's temple. We followed the noise, using the same path to the hall as before, when Menai first led me and Sebastian here.

The banquet was louder than ever and packed with Athena's followers.

But all I cared about was the fact that Violet was standing on the platform covering the pool, holding Pascal. She wore her black dress, a few sizes too big, and had a burgundy Mardi Gras mask lined with short black feathers pushed on top of her head.

Shadows curved beneath her round eyes. Her face was small and oval. Pert nose. Pink mouth. Violet was a doll, a beautiful, dark Gothic child with a penchant for reptiles, Mardi Gras, and fruit.

Instantly her name was on my lips and I moved toward her, but Menai snagged my arm and held me back.

Violet turned and stared at me.

I met her gaze. Her expression didn't change. It was solemn, quiet, unperturbed. Only Violet could pull off that look and make you believe she meant it. A feline grin built until her lips were drawn apart and her tiny white fangs flashed in the light. I smiled back and gave her an encouraging nod while everything inside me pushed and screamed to go to her and protect her.

"Calm down," Menai snapped, digging her nails into my arm.

She was right. Play it cool. Assess the area, find the guards, note the open paths, and—

Sebastian.

He stood behind Athena, his hand on the back of her chair. He was staring at me. Had been the entire time, I realized. A blank, gray stare I couldn't read.

Sebastian looked fresh, clean, more striking than I'd ever seen him look. The natural red in his lips was deeper; his gray eyes were brighter; his hair was blacker and glossier, like black satin. He possessed all the tortured beauty of a poet, all the power and elegance of a Lamarliere, all the edge and creativity of a musician. And now he could add blood-drinker to that list.

Two gods, I guessed from their looks, with regal bearing and Greek-style clothing, sat on Athena's right, while a strange-looking female occupied the left. Her skin was two different colors—right side a ghostly white and left side an inky black. The light grayish blue of her eyes was accentuated by the colors of her skin.

Athena set her cup down and stood, looking gorgeous and utterly sadistic in her dark, muted green bodysuit made from the skin of the Titan, Typhon. She hadn't dressed to impress; she'd dressed to instill fear in everyone. The reptilian hide lived, and it moved around her body, still one moment, sliding around the next. She'd worn it the first time we'd clashed in Josephine Arnaud's ballroom.

Her hair was down, loose in places and braided in others. She wore black eye makeup smudged to gray, making the green of her eyes seem brighter. She clapped her hands. The music died and the room went quiet. "Our entertainment has arrived."

Twenty-Three

The guests clapped and banged their cups on the table. Athena basked in the glow of their attention and excitement, but only for a moment. She motioned for silence. "To celebrate my Panathenaea, I give to you"—she waved her hands at the three gods, then bestowed a motherly smile on me—"the gorgon. Just a baby, really."

The two gods seated on her right went pale, glancing at each other in confusion and fear. The other one didn't have an outward reaction at all. Just like Sebastian, still and seemingly unaffected.

"Athena," a blond god said, "you bring a god-killer before us?"

"Rest easy, brother. She is not matured. I simply bring her

before you as a show of . . . good faith." The lies flowed easily from Athena's red lips; it was more like a show of strength. If Athena held the god-killer, it was yet another reason for the gods to fear her. She conveniently seemed to forget that *she* was the one who had inadvertently created the gorgons to begin with, that *she* gave us the ability to kill the gods.

Athena was so full of bullshit. I wondered if I was the only one who could see through her lies and showmanship.

"I thought it would be fun to watch her submit to my rule. The threat of the god-killer has come to an end."

My fingers flexed and then settled into tight fists. I stood out in the open, at the mercy of not one god, but four. In fact, the room was full of beings that could rip me to shreds in a matter of seconds.

I'd go down fighting. That much I knew, and I'd give everything I had to try to get my hands around Athena's neck.

The pleased look on Athena's face made me uneasy, though. *Don't panic. Remember what Bran taught you. Strike first, ask questions later*. So far I'd only been able to deliver small doses of my power that were easily countered by Athena, Bran, Menai. . . . What I needed was a powerhouse strike that filled a body so completely there'd be no way to overcome it, but I didn't even know if I could do that or if my "immaturity" even allowed it.

Athena lifted her chin and scanned the crowd. Then she

glanced down and smiled warmly at Sebastian. That little gesture was just for me. What a bitch.

"It's time," she said, her attention settling on Violet and then fixating on me with extreme malice, "for a new, revised model to destroy the old."

She raised her arms and began to speak, not in Greek, but in something far older, something that snapped through the air, the words holding energy and power.

The gods glanced from one to another, completely unsettled. One of them stood and gripped the table. "Sister, what you're doing . . . this is madness."

Just like in my vision, when I'd ingested the bones of Alice Cromley and seen the making of Medusa into the gorgon, Athena's words floated out from her as a living thing, shadows that curled and twisted and tangled.

Oh God. Athena meant to turn Violet into a gorgon.

"NO!" I lunged before Menai or the guards could stop me, leaping onto the platform and grabbing Violet, pulling her down into my lap as I slid on my rear end. I turned my back toward Athena, shielding Violet with my body and the fall of my loose hair.

Violet turned in my arms to look up at me. "Ari," she said, strangely calm for what was happening.

"Violet. Are you okay?"

She nodded. "It's okay, you know. Trust me."

Her demeanor was so odd, I blinked, unsure of what to say. She gave me a confident nod and then grinned, revealing her tiny fangs. Why the hell was she smiling?

Christ. Maybe I was still back in the cell, hallucinating.

Violet removed herself from my hold. She bent down, placed Pascal in my lap, and then pulled down her mask like a knight preparing to charge. She folded her hands in front of her, looking so small and fragile, and faced a now-silent Athena.

But the words of the curse had life; they wrapped around Violet, picking her off the platform, spinning around her in a slow, macabre dance.

I scrambled off the platform and ran for Athena, but the guards were on me in a flash, tackling me to the ground and then delivering a few choice kicks to my midsection before yanking me upright to watch.

Violet's arms raised, her tiny body stiff and frozen, her toes pointed to the ground as the words swirled around her—angry, shadowy things.

Then, very slowly, she was set on her feet.

The temple was quiet. A lone cough sounded like thunder.

Violet shoved her mask up to rest atop her head. She stood on the platform all alone, tiny and dark with her black eyes staring calmly at Athena.

Several seconds ticked by.

Nothing was happening. She wasn't changing, wasn't affected at all.

I whipped my head around to see Athena waiting for her curse to manifest, but a faint look of confusion passed over her features. It should've happened by now like it had happened with Medusa.

Now. Strike now.

With every bit of strength I had in me, I jerked from the guard's hold, using the momentum to swing back and slam my elbow into his face. Then I grabbed his arm and flipped him. As soon as his back hit the floor, I snatched the hilt of his blade, dragging it out of his sheath and taking off at a run.

I made it to Athena's table, leaped onto it, and then pushed off with all my might, aiming straight for the goddess.

My arms closed around her and we tumbled to the marble floor. Before she could recover, I rose up and slammed the hilt of the blade into her throat. It gave me enough time to roll off her and maneuver the blade properly. Her eyes went wide and she grabbed her throat, gasping. I swung the blade downward. She threw both hands out, caught it between her palms, and shoved it back, knocking me off balance.

A sword appeared out of nowhere in her hand as she stood.

Steel struck steel.

No one helped her. But then, no one would dare. She was better than me—no shocker. I ducked, just missing her blade as it arced down to sever my shoulder. It cracked the stone floor instead as I spun and swept my leg into the back of her knees, tipping her off balance.

I lunged, snagging a handful of hair at the back of her head. I was fighting for my life and I knew it. She grabbed my hand and twisted her body around until we were face-to-face. Her green eyes took on a savage light. Then she head-butted me.

Pain shot through my face, blinding me. I stumbled back as warm blood gushed from my nose and down my mouth. I sucked some of it in as I opened my mouth to breathe, making me choke on my own blood.

Athena's hand curled around my throat. She walked me backward, up the dais steps, to stand before her throne and give everyone a view of her victory. She lifted me off the floor by my neck. My windpipe squished. Stars danced in my vision. I kicked, gasping for air like a fish out of water.

She brought me closer, forgetting I still held the blade in my hand. "Nice try."

"Thanks," I forced out in a whisper, shoving the blade into her gut.

Released, I hit the dais steps and rolled onto the floor, righting myself as she removed the blade from her body and then flung it at the guard who once held it. It stuck into his skull, killing him instantly.

She'd done in the cemetery. She made a motion toward Sebastian, and he flew from the guards who were holding him and into the seat of the throne.

Then she gazed out over the hall, where her living curse still coiled and slithered above the platform like smoke in the air. With harsh, demanding words, she pulled the curse back toward her and then sent it with the flick of a hand to Sebastian, using the same powerful language as before.

The curse hadn't worked on Violet, so now she was after Sebastian. But unlike with Violet, the curse attacked him, the words swirling viciously around him, shooting into his body, making him writhe in pain. He grabbed the arms of the chair, knuckles turning white.

"Stop it!" I shrieked at the top of my lungs. "Please stop!"

I scrambled up the steps, heart pounding, electric with panic as the power inside me uncoiled like an angry serpent. *Don't think, just strike.* I grabbed his ankle, staring up at him as he gazed down, his face screwed into a deep frown at the grim realization that he could do nothing to stop this.

"I'm sorry." I closed my eyes and let my walls crumble, releasing the monster inside me, giving up control. This wasn't fighting. It was different—hope, love, sacrifice, the absence of fear. . . .

Energy ballooned, pushing against my skin, wanting out, and this time I welcomed it with everything I had.

It was dark energy, violent and alive. It hummed, a shivery path from every part of my body, down my arm and into my hand. I forced it all into Sebastian.

I lost all sense of time and place, existing in a bright void of mind-numbing ancient power.

When I finally came to, my sobs were so loud they echoed through the quiet hall. I still held on to Sebastian's ankle, but my hand was asleep and my body weak and empty.

I didn't want to look, but my gaze went to him anyway.

Oh God.

Sebastian was white marble. Beautiful. Frightening. Stone.

Twenty-Four

I couldn't get enough air into my lungs as I tried to process what I had done. Sebastian sat there on his throne as though carved by Michelangelo himself. Hands curled around the edges of the chair, face frowning down at me, hair falling over his brow, legs spread apart . . . Like some troubled young king, lost in his own tormented thoughts.

Athena leaned against the side of the throne next to Sebastian's. A broad grin split her face. Her arm was draped over the back and she drummed her fingers on the gilded surface.

The other gods stared at me in shocked realization. They now knew what I could do, knew that I was different, that Athena hadn't quite been truthful about her "baby gorgon." Now would have been the perfect time for me to grab her, to do to her what I'd done to Sebastian, but I was tapped out. I had nothing left.

Athena bent down, slipped a finger through my hair, and curled it around and around. "I knew it," she whispered with an odd note of pride. "I knew you could do it. You've done so well, Aristanae, so well. . . ."

She glanced across the expanse of the hall to the alcove with the statue of Zeus, and then her eyes swept over the banquet, gleaming with victory and anticipation.

"Feast well, for once we've had our fill"—her words rang with a powerful echo—"we take our Procession to New 2!"

The place erupted. Cups slammed on tables. Creatures roared and cheered. The sound was deafening.

Athena clapped her hands and signaled for louder music and more food. "Eat, Aristanae!" she called to me with laughter in her voice.

I frowned in confusion. One second she was fighting me, the next she wanted me to eat. She'd orchestrated this down to a T, and I'd showed her the extent of my power, used every bit of it to the point that I couldn't even turn a gnat to stone.

"Enjoy the food, the company. . . ." She gestured down one of the long tables to where Menai stood with the cloaked figure I now knew was my father.

I didn't react; I was still in shock. Athena waved at two

guards, and they grabbed me under my armpits from behind and dragged me away, my legs sliding over the floor.

And all I saw was Sebastian getting farther and farther away.

Sebastian. So beautiful. So cold. I saved him. Yes, I saved him. Hadn't I? *Oh God. What have I done?*

And then Violet came into view, walking behind me with two guards escorting her. She was holding Pascal, crying, and she was angry, her face mottled red. Crying for Sebastian, I knew.

The guards dumped me at one of the long benches.

A place had been made for me at the table, and it wasn't until I was sitting that I realized I rubbed shoulders with my father. Menai didn't join us, and instead moved back against the wall. Unsure of what to do or how to snap out of it, I placed my hands flat on the table on either side of my plate.

I sat there until the shock of what I'd done to Sebastian lessened. I started to tremble and bitterness settled into my bones.

Violet's tiny hand slipped into mine. Her chin jutted out and her expression was fierce. I gave her a miserable attempt at a smile. "I'm sorry, Vi," I whispered.

"Is Bastian . . . dead?"

"Michel can fix this," I promised. "The Novem, they have the knowledge to bring him back." They had to. Because if they didn't . . . Confusion warped my thoughts. Why? Why had I done this? Deep down in my subconscious it had felt right, the right decision. I had saved him. I'd done what some elemental part of me, some level I didn't understand, urged me to do. But now I wondered if I'd been wrong.

Time passed. Everything hurt. Everything shriveled and burned until I felt like a husk made of ashes, and the slightest breeze blew bits of me away into nothing.

A rough hand settled over mine. I turned to my father. The hood kept his face hidden. White, puckered scars and bites covered his hand and wrist, but none of that mattered. My father was here. He was touching me, holding my hand.

"I don't know what to say to you," I blurted out. What was I supposed to say? *Sorry I left you in Athena's prison before. Been wondering about you all my life. How the hell are you?*

"We have much to say, you and I," he said slowly, "but now is not the time or place." His hand squeezed mine tighter. "You"—he paused to clear his throat—"you were just a babe when I was taken."

My father had done the unthinkable by loving my mother instead of killing her as his duty commanded. Together, they had fled to New 2, and Athena had come after them, whipping the Twin Sister hurricanes into a supernatural frenzy. After promising them refuge, the Novem had turned on my parents and handed my father over to Athena in exchange for her promise to leave the city and never return. Of course, that promise hadn't lasted. . . .

"I never thought I'd see you grown," he said.

And I'd never imagined back in my pre–New 2 days that I would meet my father under these circumstances. All my life I'd wanted to know my family and what it'd be like to have real parents, and yet I found myself not wanting him to say more. Not here. Not like this.

"Why is she letting us sit together?" I asked instead.

"She is training you, Ari. Rewarding you. All her machinations have been to determine your worth. Worthy of killing or worthy of keeping as a weapon. For what end purpose, I don't know, but this is what she does. She breaks people and then uses them like pets. And she is showing off in front of her guests, letting them know she does not fear you."

"Who are they?" I nodded toward the gods at Athena's table.

"Artemis. Apollo. The ghostly one is Melinoe, daughter of Hades."

He leaned closer to me and the volume of his voice dropped. "Listen to me, Ari. Athena is not done with you yet. I have known her long and known her well. Whatever goal or plan she has is not finished."

A servant leaned forward and filled my glass.

"You'd do well to eat and drink," he suggested. "The night is far from over."

How could I eat when Sebastian was a marble statue presiding over the hall?

Still, he was right, so I broke off a chunk of bread and shoved it into my mouth. "You think I have a chance in hell of killing her?" I watched Athena feasting and conversing with the gods at her table.

"There is no one stronger. No one smarter than she," he said, and my hopes started to sink. "She is always steps ahead of those who wish her harm. Yet you continue to surprise her. As does Violet, for reasons I can't quite figure out."

"Great. So surprises aside, we're screwed."

"There is one thing she cannot foresee, and that is the extent of your abilities. The curse has been passed to you from your mother, but you are my daughter as well, and that makes you different, perhaps beyond what you've shown tonight."

"What do you mean?"

He lifted his other hand just barely to show me the hilt of a weapon peeking from beneath his sleeve. His hands curled around it. "You are a hunter, Ari. Each τέρας hunter, each Son of Perseus, excels in perception, focus, stealth, and accuracy. We *are* the weapon. Every hunter carries a blade forged with his own blood. It makes him strong, always accurate, always deadly. The blades can become extensions of our power, imbued with it. Most hunters see no need to invoke this power, for they are strong in their own right. My blood is in my blade, Ari. *Our* blood," he said, almost breathlessly.

Goose bumps rose on my skin. "What are you saying?"

"I'm saying use my blade when the time comes. Make it an extension of your power." His hand withdrew back under the sleeve of the cloak. "No more talk," he said as several guards walked by us.

We fell into silence as the feast carried on. My thoughts ran wild—when would he give me the blade, how would I use it with my power, and how the hell was I going to get Violet and my father out of here?

When Athena rose to prepare for the Procession, I saw my chance. She sent guards to collect us, and then she swept regally from the room with the gods in tow. We were escorted from the main hall and down the long corridor, which led to the prison.

My father walked behind me, a guard on either side of him. I was in the middle with two guards to keep me company, and Violet was in the front with a pair of guards flanking her.

Six guards. One semitrained gorgon. A wounded Son of Perseus. And a fanged child.

Wonderful.

As I made a quick plan of attack a soft whoosh sounded, and one of Violet's guards jerked as an arrowhead appeared out of the back of his neck. Before the guards—or even I, for that matter—could react, several more arrows were let loose, finding homes in Violet's remaining guard and my two—all struck through the throat so they couldn't utter a word.

Menai stood far down the hall. She stepped out of the shadows, another arrow notched in her bow and her sights set behind me.

My father's guards had not been hit yet and would sound the alarm. Shit. I spun to attack, but drew up short and completely stunned as Henri finished snapping the last one's neck from behind—the other guard already dead on the floor.

"Henri," I choked.

His gaze lifted. Wild, predatory eyes burned fiercely. His hair was loose and tangled, and he looked horrible.

I ran and flung myself against him, hugging him and wanting to make sure he was real. "Oh, thank God. You're alive," I said, stating the obvious.

He hissed in pain. "Stop squeezing!"

I drew back immediately as fresh blood stained his dirty shirt. "Oh shit, you're still hurt. I'm sorry."

"Talk later," my father said. "We must dispose of the bodies."

Menai, Henri, and my father dragged the guards into a room off the hallway and removed the arrows so they couldn't be identified.

Violet hadn't moved since the guards had dropped dead on either side of her. "Violet." I knelt in front of her. She blinked and looked at me. "Are you okay?"

She nodded, holding Pascal tightly to her. "I want to go home now."

I grabbed her hand as the others gathered around. "We need to get back to the gate in the old temple. Menai, is there a way to get to the lake from here?"

"Yes, follow me."

Menai led us toward the prison and veered off into a narrow corridor. We ran flat out. My lungs were on fire. At one point I ended up carrying Violet so we could move even faster.

And then we were outside on the rocks just below the wall of Athena's garden. The wind howled and pushed at us as we hugged the cliff face. I glanced at Henri to see how he was doing. Not good. He held his side. His face was damp and sickly pale.

"There," Menai said, pointing to a treacherous cliff path. We were so high up that a few thin clouds floated parallel with us in the distance. As we set off I realized Menai hadn't moved. "You're not coming?"

"I can't. I must return to the hall. This is as far as I go."

"Come with us."

She backed away. "You don't understand. I have to go back. Good-bye, Ari."

I did understand to a degree. It was pretty obvious Athena had something on her, some reason to make Menai stay by her side. "Menai." She stopped. "Thank you."

"Yeah, well, just don't make me regret it."

"I won't."

Once we'd picked our way over the narrow cliffside path, we climbed the rocks to reach the lake, and then it was a familiar journey around the lake and into the dark woods before we finally emerged near the eerie, ghostly garden of stone statues.

I hung back as Henri, Violet, and my father walked up the steps of Athena's deserted temple. My father paused halfway up. "Ari. Hurry."

The two people I'd come here to save stood ready to go, and yet I didn't move. I couldn't.

Making my decision, I drew in a deep breath and spoke. "Henri, take Violet and my father back to the gate."

His mouth opened, then closed, and then he just stared hard at me as my father came down the steps and grabbed my hands. I knew what he'd say. This was a chance for us. We were moments away from freedom.

"I have to go back," I told him. "This isn't over."

I thought he'd argue, thought he'd play the father card and demand I go with them, but he did neither of those things. He handed me his blade, and I had a feeling I was really going to like my dad.

A soft, sad laugh escaped me as I felt its weight in my hands and, oddly, the faint hum of its power. The other τέρας blades hadn't felt that way, but then, those weren't forged with my father's blood. I handed it back, not wanting to risk it being confiscated. "Take it with you. Find me when the Procession comes to New 2, and I might just be able to do something with that blade of yours."

He took it back and slid it under his cloak. Then he cradled my face in his scarred hands. His face remained shadowed by his hood, but I saw enough to know that his eyes were bright with pride. "You are a true hunter, with a warrior's heart and your mother's spirit. I will wait for you in New 2." And then he kissed me on the head and walked up the stairs to wait at the top.

That might've been the nicest and coolest thing anyone had ever said to me, and it hurt like hell, the sadness and regret of our situation burning a hole in my heart.

Henri came down, holding his side. Blood made wet lines between his fingers.

"Fix that scratch," I said, gesturing to his wound. "Then go to Bran and Michel and tell them Athena is coming to the city." I moved forward to hug him gently. "And guard my father. I need him."

"Consider it done, *mon amie*."

"And, Henri?" I paused, trying to find the right words, something more than "thank you"; after what he'd been through, "thank you" fell short.

"Don't sweat it. You'll be owing me for years to come."

Then Violet was there, launching her dark little self into my arms.

"I'm sorry," I whispered into her hair, "for what happened, for everything."

She reared back and smiled at me, those tiny fangs flashing in the moonlight. "We're going to make Athena wish she'd never been born, Ari." She said it so evenly and so bluntly that I almost believed her. She hugged me again. "Hurry home."

"Will do."

She walked up the steps, picked up Pascal, and then took Henri's hand. They turned with my father and disappeared into the blackness of the temple.

Weary, I walked up to the top step and sat down. I was alone. In the dark. Whatever happened now, at least they were safe. And I knew I'd be going home very soon thanks to Athena; there was no way in hell her ego would let her leave me behind. She'd want to show me off, make the Novem think they'd lost me.

I stood, squaring my shoulders. A breeze picked up. I pushed my hair from my eyes so I could stare across the lake. Zeus's perfect temple shone like a beacon, its fires glittering on the water. The sounds of music and voices carried over the surface. The contrast of what I saw and where I stood made my lips quirk into a smile.

I was in moonlight and shadow, a broken temple rising up behind me. Broken but still standing. Like me.

The warm wind caressed my skin. A deep sense of purpose and serenity filled me, and I stayed there for a moment soaking it in, letting it fill every part of me. And then I went down the steps and headed back through the garden of stone, no longer terrified of the eerie statues, but sad. They reminded me of what needed to be done. This would be the last place like this ever to exist. *It ends with me.*

I went around the fallen warhorse I'd seen earlier and passed the mother and her child. I stopped and stared at the prison of marble they found themselves in.

The child in the blanket had been loved, it seemed. Its plump arm hung out in a relaxed manner. The mother's expression appeared so frightened, her white marble eyes wide. And the poor kid couldn't have been more than two or three. Frozen. An entire life stolen.

Time pressed in on me. Once I hit twenty-one and became a full-blown gorgon, anyone who met my gaze would be history. I wouldn't even have to touch them. I didn't want this! Yet I didn't seem to have much choice. This mother and child, they'd had no choice either.

I reached out and grabbed the child's chubby hand, my chest aching. My eyes fell closed and I found myself offering a silent apology. *Sorry. I'm so sorry.*

The weight of my sorrow wasn't only for the child but for

all the victims of the gorgons, for my ancestors, my father, my friends, and everyone who'd been hurt because of our power. I'd make amends. I'd set the wrongs to right. I had to. I opened my eyes and gave the child one last look.

It blinked.

A strangled scream burst from my lips as I leaped away. My ankle turned and I fell, landing on my ass, my elbows digging deep into the soft earth. I scrambled back up, heart pounding.

In one split second the child's eyes and lids had become flesh and color in a canvas of hard, weathered stone. And they'd blinked before the flesh ebbed back to marble.

Holy shit.

TWENTY-FIVE

STUNNED, I JUST STOOD THERE IN THE GARDEN GAPING AT THE stone child. I couldn't . . . that baby . . . going crazy . . . like my mother . . . But deep down the gorgon in me had known.

And then I ran, tearing through the woods.

By the time I came to the lawn, I was exhausted, panting hard, and every muscle burned. After a short rest I stuck to the wall and proceeded to Athena's pretty garden and into the banquet hall, which was filling again with armed minions and followers.

Immediately I looked for Sebastian. *No.* He was gone.

I glanced wildly around the room, over the alcove where the tall statue of Zeus stood, past the columns, and—

Everything came to a grinding halt. I looked back at the

statue. Athena had killed Zeus. No one knew why or what had started the war. There was an infant fated to kill him, an infant that statue in the alcove had once held in its hands.

Why would she keep the statue of her father? If I walked over to it and touched it, would a creepy zing shoot through my hand?

I'd bet my life it would.

Athena marched into the room wearing gold chain mail and armor over a short white gown that brushed the tops of her knees. The flames reflected off the gold's polished surface, making her shimmer like a star. She wore a Greek-style helmet pushed up onto her head and a round shield over her back. Sandals laced all the way up her bare calves.

"The gate has been prepared?" she asked one of her minions. He nodded. "Good. Let's give the Novem a show they'll never forget, shall we?"

She swept by as though I wasn't even worth a glance. A guard grabbed my arm and shoved me out of the hall, down the temple steps, and into the enormous courtyard.

I almost stumbled when I saw Sebastian on a raised platform at the back of a large float. The front of the float resembled a golden chariot; two massive white bulls stomped their feet and snorted, making the entire thing rock.

We were going into New 2 with Sebastian as a message for

the Novem, for Michel. A show of her power. Her own little Mardi Gras parade. Athena was a tyrannical, highly intelligent lunatic. She leaped onto the float and grabbed the reins, looking like some Amazon queen.

Guards lifted me onto the float. Chains were attached to metal rings on the floorboards. They manacled my wrists and ankles with enough length that I could stand if I wanted to, but for now I sat.

The courtyard was packed. Bloodlust and the thrill of battle grew until the air felt charged. The float rocked as the bulls fidgeted.

Menai appeared near the right side of the float, walking alongside as it began to move. Her quiver was packed with arrows, and several blades covered her person. Ahead of us, between two enormous columns, were familiar blood symbols. I knew there were two more just like that at the bottom.

This was a gate like the one in Entergy Tower, but this was on a grand scale, bigger and able to fit an entire legion. I had a feeling Athena and her minions had made this kind of march many times over the ages.

I glanced over my shoulder. Sebastian's marble form loomed above me; we were in almost the same position we'd been in when I'd turned him to stone. Now it seemed he was looking right at me. "We're going home, Sebastian," I whispered.

❖ ❖ ❖

Bonfires raged along Loyola Avenue, the light reflecting off the high-rises and every piece of exposed glass and metal, making the area glow.

The rubble and trash had been pushed to the edges of the street to make a clear path for the Procession. There was no audience yet, but they'd come. It was only a matter of time before the Novem got wind of our arrival. The Procession was prepared for an inevitable battle, and Athena couldn't wait to show off her acquisitions.

Once Michel saw his son, the shit was going to hit the fan.

Once he realized it was me who'd turned Sebastian to stone . . . I might just be a goner.

I watched and waited, scanning the gutted buildings and side streets, hoping a few familiar faces lurked in the shadows.

Fires burst ahead of us to light our way.

A flash caught my attention. Eyes gleamed from the blackness of a building . . . unfriendly eyes. The more we progressed, the more I saw. A few turnskins hovered out in the open, standing atop the rubble piles, their heads hung low between bony shoulder blades, totally captivated with the fresh meat parading by. Revenants, too, followed our slow path by jumping from one building to the next.

Ahead of us a turnskin boldly attacked one of Athena's minions and tried to pull him into a parking deck. The canine turnskin was torn to shreds by the minion within seconds. It was a brutal, vicious display.

A faint cry overhead made me glance up. A large bird banked to the left, its wings wide and its tail feathers long.

Henri.

Athena studied me over her gold-plated shoulder. "It won't be long now," she said.

I gave her a belligerent look. "Long for what? More of you showing off? I'm tired of your stupid games, Athena. I don't care what you do."

She laughed at my dishonesty and angled more to face me. "All my *games* have a purpose. I do nothing without cause. And this one"—she looked beyond me at nothing—"has been a long time coming."

She turned her back to me and pulled on the reins.

The chains dragged across the float as I pushed to my feet. The Novem had come, forming a line in the street up ahead. We were near the outer edges of the ruins now.

A slow stream of adrenaline began building in my system. Quickly I skimmed the crowd, looking for help or an opportunity. Menai still stood by the float, and behind her was a tall, cloaked form with broad shoulders.

My father. I knew that cloak. Somehow he'd fallen in with us.

A scan of the area showed several Novem on the rooftops.

And—a smile erupted inside me—one familiar harpy perched on the corner of a tall office building.

Mapsaura had come. I'd freed her from Athena's prison, and in return she'd aided me during the cemetery battle with Athena. Now, thank God, she was here again.

Goose bumps raced along my arms and thighs. Her large leathery wings were folded back and her claws curled around the ledge. She looked like an imposing gargoyle sitting up there. I'd heard rumors that she'd taken up in the ruins—good hunting grounds, apparently.

Her presence filled me with hope. The minions in front of us parted, allowing the float to continue to the front line. Athena halted the bulls. It was close enough to the Novem that I could see the top of Josephine's head and part of Michel's face. Behind them stood Gabriel and the other Novem heirs in his clique.

Bran was at the end of the Novem line. The sight of him, feet braced apart, arms folded over his chest like usual, and what looked like a massive broadsword strapped to his back, brought an instant smile to my face.

He caught my eye. One of his eyebrows lifted as if to say, *Selkirk, I'm unimpressed.*

I gave him an innocent shrug because I knew he'd roll his eyes, which he did. Then he dismissed me and scowled at Athena.

"What do you think of my parade? It's very Mardi Gras, don't you think?" Athena called to the Novem, moving aside to present her spoils. "You like my statue? I think he takes after you, Michel."

With her out of the way, the Novem line had full view of Sebastian on the platform behind me. Michel's gray eyes went from Athena to the statue. His son. The son he'd finally been reunited with after a decade. I winced at the horror in his eyes.

The shit's going to hit the fan. The shit's going to hit the fan.

Michel took one large step forward. "What have you done?!" he shouted, and I wasn't sure if he was talking to me or Athena.

"Ah!" Athena wagged a finger at him. "Not yet. We have a bit of bargaining to do if you want your heir back." She tilted her head to Josephine. "Or is he *your* heir, Josephine? He has taken blood, you know. He's an Arnaud now. A double heir. It'd be tragic to lose him."

Josephine went pale. For the first time since I'd met her, she seemed truly dismayed. She moved up to stand united with Michel. "What do you want?"

"You know exactly what I want," Athena snarled. The exchange between them was personal, and it didn't surprise me at all. If anyone had their hands in something dirty and wrong, it'd be Josephine.

"We will give her nothing!" Michel bellowed in pain, his eyes bright with it, the veins on his temple angry and enlarged. "In return for what? A son who can never be?"

"Oh, I think you'd be surprised what can *be*, Michel. And besides, you're the great and powerful Novem. I thought you could do anything. Wouldn't you rather have him than, say . . . me dropping him off a fifty-story building?"

Dread sliced down my spine. Energy was gathering. I couldn't tell from where.

"What do you want, Athena?" Josephine demanded, a hard edge to her tone.

"I WANT THE DAMN JAR BACK!" she shouted in full-blown anger. A wave of oppressive energy wafted over the area and shook the ground. Just as suddenly as it manifested, it was gone again, and her voice returned to normal. "Take what you have stored there. Leave that which was inside when you received it. A simple trade. Take it or leave it."

Josephine's eyes narrowed. But the other Novem heads looked as though they had no idea why Athena would want Anesidora's Jar or its original contents. The legendary jar, Pandora's Box, had been given to the ancestors of the Novem so long ago, who knew what might've been inside when it was handed over. But I bet the Keeper knew. I bet I knew too.

I could see Josephine's mind working. Whatever Athena

wanted was leverage. It could be powerful. It could be something that lifted Josephine and the Arnaud family to new heights.

Sebastian, though, was the wild card. Josephine cared for him in her own weird way, and he represented power as a double heir and now as a Mistborn vampire.

Which was more useful? Sebastian or the jar?

"And the gorgon?" Bran spoke up, nodding to me.

"She's mine," Athena stated bluntly. "So what shall it be, Josephine? Your heir in pieces, or the jar?"

The ominous air filtering into the street possessed such clarity. It crept and crawled like bugs along my psyche. Something bad was brewing, and the last thing I wanted was to be chained on some float when all hell broke loose. And now that Athena was distracted, it was time for me to act.

I regulated my breathing, closed my eyes to settle myself, and tapped into the monster within me. Just to let the gorgon out a little. There was no one I cared about being tortured, no emotional distractions to keep me from focusing, no starvation or weakness. I could do this.

I grabbed the chains below each of my manacled wrists, glancing quickly to Bran, his faint nod giving me confidence. As Athena and the Novem discussed the trade, I concentrated on calling up my power and turning the chains to stone.

The memory of standing alone on the steps of Athena's ruined temple filled my mind. The dark temple looming behind me, the breeze stirring my hair, the lake, and the stone garden. The sense of calm. The call to arms that stirred in my chest.

I knew who I was. I hadn't realized it then, but I'd accepted it.

My skin buzzed. Heat poured down my arms as darkness uncoiled, snaking under my skin, a serpent made of shadows and ancient energy. I shuddered even as I envisioned it, told it where to go and what to do. My hands went numb. My fingers squeezed tightly on the chains.

The metal cracked like ice.

I released my focus and looked down, breathing heavily. The metal had become stone. My heart beat wildly. I still needed to do the chains attached to my ankles. My gaze caught on Menai. She stared at the stone. Then she looked purposefully away.

Athena remained intent on negotiations, on how to exchange the jar, the condition it must be in, the condition Sebastian must be in. They left nothing to chance.

Suddenly the hairs on the back on my neck stood. Some of the τέρας on the outer edges of the lines glanced around warily. I peered into the darkness, knowing they were out there, the creatures of the ruins. The revenants, turnskins, loups-garous, and whatever the hell else lurked in this war zone.

The scent of live flesh and blood drew them here.

Menai notched an arrow, pointing downward; she was wary as her head turned toward the buildings. Bran's sword was out of its sheath. But he, too, held his weapon down, hands curled around the hilt, the tip of the blade stuck into the pavement.

And then the shit hit the fan.

Twenty-Six

A sudden rush of wind blew over the Procession. Everyone near the float ducked in reaction as Mapsaura plucked Athena's helmet off her head. The harpy lifted her prize and dipped her head to put it on. As soon as the helmet touched down, Mapsaura disappeared.

Within a second of the theft Bran was on the float swinging his great sword down toward Athena's head. She had little time to react, her blade barely making it up in time to stop Bran's sword from severing her head. The attack set off a chain reaction, triggering the kill instincts in the creatures of the ruins. They fell on the τέρας and the Novem on three sides.

Shouts and fighting and power filled the street. The float

lurched wildly as a turnskin leaped onto the back of one of the white bulls and bit. Red flowed over white. Athena and Bran lost their balance. Michel was fighting his way to the float.

A gigantic loup-garou tore through Athena's minions like they were nothing, heading in my direction.

Shit. I pulled the chain at one wrist taut and then stomped down, breaking the stone in half. The loup-garou closed in. Now my arm was free, but still manacled and still with several stone links attached. Frantic, I broke the other chain as the werewolf-like creature leaped onto the float.

My ankles still chained, I swung my arms around, using the stone links as weapons. The chains swung around and cracked him in the side of the face. His skull dented in, and he went flying off the float along with a few busted links.

"Ari!"

I turned at the sound of my father's shout. He'd gotten sucked out away from the float. He withdrew his blade, flipped it hilt first, and then lobbed it like a football toward me.

"Menai!" Athena shouted, her attention on the blade arcing through the air.

In less than a second Menai strung another arrow and aimed it at the blade. She was going to knock it off course. Athena was right there. Menai wouldn't openly disobey her like this.

"NO!" I jerked at the manacles on my ankles.

She let the arrow fly. It soared through the air, lightning fast, knocking my father's blood-forged blade from its perfect arc toward me. Athena shouted more commands as she fought against Bran.

One of Athena's harpies dove for the blade. She caught it in her talons and then pushed higher into the air.

My hopes sank. Until the harpy flew sideways and rolled in midair, hit by something unseen. Mapsaura? I could hear the flapping of leathery wings, but I saw nothing as the harpy screeched and fought, and—oh God—dropped the blade.

I screamed, pulling so hard on the chains that the manacles cut into my ankles. I had to get that blade, and I'd never do that stuck on the float. A hawk zoomed past me so quick and close, my hair puffed. His red tail flashed past my vision.

Henri. He plucked the blade from the air, banked, came arcing back toward the float, and dropped the blade. I caught it by the hilt. Power hummed in my hand. My thoughts and memories and emotions warped inward to form a single-minded purpose.

The blood forged into the metal ran through my veins. The blade was my conduit, my weapon, an extension of myself. I understood now what my father meant.

"Athena!" I shouted, my voice sounding far away as I lifted the blade behind my head with both hands.

All the energy and power I had, I forced upward into the blade, giving it my will and finally connecting and accepting the monster in my subconscious. Using all the strength in my body, I threw the blade as Athena spun around. It made four rotations before it slammed into the goddess, piercing her armor and sinking deep in her chest. The force knocked her back several steps. For a few seconds she seemed frozen, but then her eyes locked on me like two heat-seeking missiles.

She advanced, pulling out the blade. Her other hand grabbed my throat. Before she could speak, I forced out, "That blade is my father's, forged with his blood, the same blood that runs though my veins. You know what it's designed to do. You're so smart, you figure it out."

I watched with satisfaction as the realization dawned on her. I'd delivered my power without ever having to touch her, and even now it was spreading out from her wound, turning the blood and armor to stone.

"You know what's funny, Athena? You created us both, the gorgons and the Sons of Perseus. And now you'll die by our power. You will harden from the inside out, and I hope it fucking hurts."

The inner gleam in her green eyes didn't dim, but instead grew brighter. Laughter bubbled to her throat and burst through her mouth with a strangled sound. "You're so . . . naive and . . . small-minded," she gasped through pain and humor.

"I'm not the one about to take her last breath."

"And I could crush your windpipe right now, stupid girl." Something shifted in her gaze, something that revealed a depth of emotion far greater than I'd ever imagined.

"But you won't," I said. "I know what you want from me."

Her eyes filled with pain. She sneered. "You know nothing. And you will always be an insignificant nothing." She shoved my father's blade into my side. Hot pain sliced through me as her lips kissed my cheek. "This isn't over. For either one of us. Enjoy your wound as I shall enjoy mine."

Athena yanked the blade out. I staggered back as my power slowly worked through her system.

My hand went to my wound. My vision wavered, from the shock and pain. She shouted something to her army, the last of her words clipped as her throat hardened.

And then she blinked out.

Gone.

Most of her army disappeared with her, leaving the Novem to fend off the creatures of the ruins.

The float lurched again as one of the bulls broke from the

harness and fled into the fray, jumping over the minions that were left behind and the Novem, crushing anything beneath its giant hooves.

The sounds of screams and explosions became muted by the fear thundering through me. The pain in my side soured my stomach, and a cold sweat broke out on my skin. I had to stay lucid. My survival depended on it.

The strength I found to lift my arms and start swinging the stone chains was one of those things fueled by survival adrenaline. I hit a revenant off the float and then a turnskin, but more were coming. The float rocked again. I stumbled. My father leaped onto the float, followed by Bran. They met back-to-back, fending off attacks. The hood slid off my father's head, revealing savage, puckered scars and missing hair and skin. He was weak, still healing, and I wanted to shout at him to go, but I didn't want to distract him and get him killed.

My arms burned as I swung the chains around and around, hitting anything that approached. Time seemed to stretch on forever. And all I could think about was getting them off the float so I could reach Sebastian before they toppled him to the hard pavement below.

I hit two more creatures. A third. I dropped my arms, and then my knees hit the floor, my lungs on fire, heart hammering. I was unable to continue. A hand slid across the surface of the float—a leathery gray hand that tossed a key toward me.

Shocked, I glanced up and saw a τέρας, an old one. He had a scar over the corner of his eye, pulling down his eyelid. And then it hit me. It was the same one caught by the Novem heirs in the Saenger Theatre. Our eyes met for a fraction of a second before he ducked down and out of sight.

I lunged for the key, grabbing it and forcing my exhausted arm muscles to stop shaking long enough to put the key into the manacle lock at my ankle. It slid in and clicked. Thank God! The second manacle came off and I ran, scrambling onto the raised platform and pulling myself up until I was standing between Sebastian's knees and throwing my arms around him, holding on and trying desperately to do to him what I'd done to that child back in the stone garden.

Wake! Oh God! Please wake up!

Something hit me from behind and latched on with sharp claws, which dug into my hips, piercing the flesh and pushing down. I screamed as I felt the weight and bites of several creatures as they attacked me like a pack of wild dogs.

Their weight pressed me down. I couldn't turn to fight. Claws clamped around my shoulders. I held on to Sebastian tighter. Teeth tore into my bicep, tugging back and forth in a frenzy.

I screamed, loud and raw and from a place inside me I didn't know existed.

I heard shouts behind me. I grasped Sebastian tighter. I was losing strength in the arm that was being torn to shreds, and the wound at my side weakened my consciousness. They were pulling me down. And it was all happening so fast. I cried against stone skin, wetting it with my tears. "Please, wake up. Sebastian . . . please . . . I'm sorry . . . wake up."

A claw sliced my scalp. The hold on my foot grew so strong, my leg was pulled straight. Something had my hair and jerked hard. A hand grabbed mine—a revenant had crawled up the back of the throne.

No, no, no, no . . .

From a far distance I heard my father and Bran. I thought I heard Michel shouting, but it didn't matter. It was too late for me. My arms were giving way.

A dark door opened inside me: a secret place, the place where I'd retreat to as a child when things got too overwhelming for me to handle. It was peaceful and silent. No one could reach me there. The bites and ripping flesh—that was happening to someone else now, not me. Not me.

Blackness welcomed me with open arms.

⟡ ⟡ ⟡

"Shh. I've got you," a voice said, pulling me out of the darkness. "You don't have to cry anymore."

Soft hands gathered me up.

My body throbbed with extreme, pulsating pain. The scent of blood was so strong, like a mist in the air that hit the back of my throat with each inhale.

My head fell back and I opened my eyes.

Sebastian's face came into focus. He was real and warm and beautiful. His eyes glowed like polished silver. He was standing, holding me in his arms.

"Is this real?" I whispered as he stepped off the throne's platform.

"Yes." One word. One menacing, volatile word. His attention was not on me, but somewhere else. He kicked something off the platform. The gold cuff went clattering. I let my head fall against his shoulder as he jumped off the float, landing easily and carrying me effortlessly through the battle.

Turnskins and revenants fell to the ground, their eyes bulging as we passed. They dropped like flies, a monstrous wave parting for Sebastian as though he was Death itself, clearing a path. *Surely a dream,* I thought, trying to stay conscious.

I saw Michel several feet away. He finished off an enemy I couldn't see, paused, panting and bloodied, and then stared at Sebastian in shock. His face went several shades lighter.

Sebastian stopped in front of him. "Can you handle the rest?"

Michel nodded mutely, and I wondered why they hell he looked like he'd just seen a ghost. My head lolled to one side and my vision wavered.

TWENTY-SEVEN

I WOKE IN A FAMILIAR BED. SUNLIGHT STREAMED IN FROM AN open door, and in the courtyard beyond birds chirped amid voices and laughter.

I was on the ground floor of Michel's house in the French Quarter.

There was incredible warmth at my back and the familiar scents of Sebastian's shampoo, clean skin, and something else—a note of cologne or deodorant, I wasn't sure. It was a good combination, and I drew it deep into my lungs.

I rolled slowly beneath the covers to rest on my other side, despite the stiff muscles and sore wounds.

Sebastian lay on top of the white duvet, one arm tucked beneath his head. He wore a faded black T-shirt and jeans. His eyes were closed. He had a nice profile—masculine, noble—and it made me think of the stone statue he'd become and how frighteningly beautiful it was.

But that was history, I decided. Ancient history.

He was here now. With me and alive.

His stomach rose and fell with each breath. I wanted to place my palm flat on his abdomen and feel him for myself, to make sure this wasn't a dream.

Ignoring the hurt in my arm, I reached out and pressed my pointer finger into his shoulder. The skin gave; it was soft.

I did it again, still amazed.

A slow grin tugged at his red lips, making a dimple in his cheek. "Why," he said in a sleep-deepened voice, keeping his eyes shut, "are you poking me?"

A warm glow washed over me like sunlight after a long winter; I smiled instantly.

I slid my hand under my cheek and just stared. "I'm poking you because you're real."

He turned his head, eyes opening. They were different, his eyes—stranger, more intense, a more brilliant silvery gray. And not only his eyes but everything about him was a little more vivid.

We stared at each other for a long moment.

"I am the same," he said quietly. "In my head and heart, I'm the same."

Regret came rushing in, for all that had happened to him. The torture, the fact that I'd taken his choice away from him and now he was something he never wanted to be. My eyes stung.

"Don't do that to yourself, Ari. You did what I would've done." He turned his body toward me. "There's no way in hell I'd sit there and watch you die, not when I had the means to save you."

My throat grew so thick I couldn't talk, couldn't say I was sorry. He reached over and grabbed my hand, linking his fingers with mine. Seeing them joined, our hands together, resting on his stomach, gave me a deep sense of belonging.

"I'm sorry for a lot of things too," he said. "That I lost my way, didn't help you after . . ."

I couldn't meet his gaze just then. "Why did you . . . why were you there like that in Athena's garden?"

"I was still . . . changing. If I wasn't sick, I was blood-drunk. When you saw me, I was probably high as a kite. In the hall when Athena tried to curse me, I was so out of it, hearing things from outside, seeing the smallest details, a million things coming at me at once. It was hard to pay attention." Red crept up his neck and into his face. "I needed blood constantly," he said uncomfortably, "and she—"

"Say no more." Zaria's servant had provided it, and I didn't want to hear him say it, or picture it either.

Those moments I wish I could erase forever, but the memories were as clear as day. Zaria biting him. Them together in the garden, Sebastian plucking the guitar, looking straight through me. He probably still needed blood, would forever now. But right then I didn't want to ask him the details.

"Who's outside?" I asked, changing the subject.

"Crank, Dub, Henri . . ."

"Violet?"

"Violet. And Pascal, too."

Thank God. "You know, I'm not sure Violet ever really needed rescuing. There's something strange about her." At his arched eyebrow, I laughed. "I mean more so than normal." I laughed again at the word "normal." "You know what I mean."

He thought about that for a moment. "Yeah, I do."

"And my father?"

I was almost afraid of the answer. As one of Athena's hunters, he had always been an enemy to the Novem, and a small part of me worried the Novem would toss him in prison, or maybe they already had.

"He's in the garden."

Relief washed over me. "How did he get here?"

"He followed when I brought you here and then refused to leave."

I winced. "How did Michel handle that?"

"After your dad camped in the garden the first two nights, my father finally relented and offered him a room. Theron refused, though he has been making use of the kitchen and shower and our family's healer. . . . Violet and the kids like him."

"How long have I been here?"

"Four days."

I rose up, propelled by that shocker, the blade wound in my side reacting badly to the movement. "Four days," I repeated as pain made me sway.

"Yeah. Our healer has been caring for you. The first two days she kept you in a state of sleep. The last two she has taken care of you. You don't remember?"

I frowned. Now that I thought about it, I did seem to remember being bandaged, soup running down my chin, being helped to the bathroom. "It's all blurry," I finally said.

"Here." Sebastian piled the pillows behind me. "Sit back."

I sank against the pillows, waiting for the pain to lessen.

Crank's face appeared in the open doorway, then disappeared. "Guys! She's up!"

She was back again, hurrying across the room and crawling onto the bed to hug me tightly. "I knew you'd find Vi. You're like a legend now." I laughed, grabbed her cabbie hat, and pulled it over her eyes. She settled on the foot of the bed, sitting cross-legged.

Dub and Henri came in, followed by Violet, who pulled my father along by the hand. He hesitated at the threshold. "It's okay," I said. "You can come in."

Violet released him, and Crank helped her onto the bed. "Where's Pascal?" I asked.

"In the garden."

My father hadn't moved from his spot by the door, and I suspected he was just as nervous as I was.

His cloak was gone, replaced with jeans and a blue oxford shirt rolled to his forearms. Despite the jagged scars that still marred him, he was a handsome guy with strong, classical features and blond hair that was already growing back. He looked like a fierce, battle-scarred warrior. *A retired warrior,* I thought firmly, surprised by how strongly I felt about that.

He was my father. I wanted him to have peace and happiness, a life without torture, grief, loss. . . . He'd paid his dues.

I realized I was staring and the room had gone quiet. Heat bloomed on my cheeks. "How's your scratch, Henri?" I asked.

He snorted and leaned against the dresser. "You mean the shotgun blast to my side? It's wonderful. I have about eighty pellet-size scars to show for it."

"Dude," Dub said, plopping down in one of the chairs, "who gets shot with their own gun? Embarrassing, if you ask me."

Henri gave Dub's chair a hard shove with his foot. Dub laughed, and Henri rolled his eyes.

"Look at this, Ari." Dub shook his stomach with his hands. "That's happiness right there. Michel's got a kick-ass chef. I'm talking top of the line. I think you should play sick until tomorrow. He's going to make red velvet cake. Speaking of food . . ." Dub got up and walked to the intercom panel near the door and pressed a button.

"Kitchen," a heavy French accent said through the speaker.

Dub turned to us, winked, and then leaned close to the panel. "Snow White has risen. I repeat. Snow White has risen."

"Excusez-moi?" Pause. "Is this you again, Dub?" The irritation in the tone was unmistakable. *"Nom de Dieu!"* crackled through the speaker, followed by a long string of scolding, unintelligible French words.

"Yeah. Roger that. We're going to need food. Meats, cheeses, chips, chocolate, sweet tea, beignets. Just bring it all. She's hungry."

We all burst out laughing. Even my father cracked a half smile.

After I ate, showered, and had more visitors—Michel and Bran—I finally found myself alone in the courtyard. For exercise, I walked around the rectangular lawn a few times and then into the English-style garden.

My father sat on a stone bench, elbows on his knees, head resting in his hands. He glanced up at me. I didn't move. Neither did he. We just stared at each other for a while before I mustered the courage to walk over. I felt odd sharing the bench, so I sat in the grass facing him.

In Athena's temple the threat of danger had overshadowed the nerves and awkwardness that I felt now. He didn't say anything, and I knew he was giving me time, letting me get comfortable. I picked at a blade of grass. "So what happens now?"

He thought for a moment. "I stay in New 2, find a home, and get to know my daughter. If she's willing."

I nodded. "She is."

My heart hurt with grief. Lost time. So much taken from both of us.

As though he could read my thoughts, he said in a gentle tone, "We move forward, aye?"

I smiled. "Are you trying to read me, or does it just come naturally?"

"Both. You were frowning and your eyes went sad. Your heart sped up and your scent changed subtly. Palms are about to get sweaty. . . ."

I rubbed my hands together. "That's kind of freaky. I guess you can tell if I'm lying, too." He shrugged. "So there'll be no sneaking out and lying about boys, then?" I joked.

From the look on his face, probably not something he wanted to think about.

"Your young man," he began. "You're serious about him?"

I'd totally opened the door to that one, and since I had, I decided to be honest. "Yeah. I like him." I left it at that, wondering how my father felt about me dating Michel Lamarliere's son.

"Sebastian and Henri came with you through Athena's gate," he said, as if that explained it all. And I supposed it did. "They are both . . . acceptable."

I laughed at that. If only he knew Henri and his penchant for getting under everyone's skin. "Are you trying to steer me away from Sebastian? Because he's Michel's son?"

"No, Ari. You have made your own way, made your own choices, and I am . . . proud of the woman you've become. Sebastian seems to care a great deal for you."

"But?"

"He is powerful. Disturbingly so."

Then we make a good pair, I thought, because I was pretty disturbing to people too. My father wasn't exaggerating, though. Sebastian, being Mistborn and now a full-blown vampire, had displayed some horrifying new abilities after I'd resurrected him from stone. Creatures dropping dead as he passed. . . .

It was no more than two hours ago, during my visit with Bran and Michel, that I'd learned Sebastian had simply commanded the creatures of the ruins in his mind: *Stop breathing.*

And that's what they'd done. They'd suffocated themselves.

Because he'd *told* them to.

His powers of persuasion were amplified to a degree no one had ever seen before.

Now I understood why he'd told me his mind and heart hadn't changed. He wanted me to see beyond the horror of what he'd done, that he wasn't going to let it change who he was, wasn't going to let it go to his head.

I picked some more grass. "So what do you think happened to Athena?"

"I think she went back to her temple, did whatever she could to halt the power you set free within her. If she did survive, she is in terrible pain. Only you can reverse what has already been done."

"And Menai? Do you think she's okay?"

My father let out a deep sigh. "Menai is resourceful. She'll be fine. She will never leave Athena. Not until the goddess is dead."

"What does Athena have on her?"

"Artemis. Menai fears what Athena will do to her mother. Though the what or the why of it, I don't know. She would never say."

"I should have known," I said. The bow, her accuracy, it should've been a dead giveaway.

I could only hope that Athena had become as hard and cold

as granite and Menai had dropped her over the garden wall to smash on the rocks below.

"Come, dinner will be ready soon."

I didn't smell a thing, but my father was standing and holding out a hand to me. I glanced up at him with a lopsided smile. "What's on the menu?"

He turned his face toward the house and drew in a deep breath. "Pork chops stuffed with corn bread and andouille sausage, crawfish étouffée . . . a spinach salad with praline-crusted bacon."

I laughed and he smiled broadly. His face transformed, and I knew then why my mother had fallen head over heels for him. I slid my hand into his and let him pull me to my feet.

"May I?" he asked, lifting our hands. He didn't want to let go.

Something light and good sank into my heart and settled there with a sigh. I nodded, and together we walked toward the house.

Twenty-Eight

Sebastian and I sat high above Jackson Square on the wide ledge surrounding the middle steeple of St. Louis Cathedral. Below us the square was lit up with its usual nighttime revelry. Jazz wafted on the breeze along with the hum of conversation and laughter.

Two days had passed since my conversation in the garden with my father. And I'd just spent the last few hours in the library trying to find out if there was more information about the witch who could untangle my curse.

I wanted my curse lifted. Sure, I might be different from any other gorgon before me, but no one knew what would happen when I turned twenty-one. I might still turn into a full-blown gorgon. I'd no longer look like me, and I'd no longer be able to meet anyone's gaze without turning them to stone. And I sure as hell wasn't going to sit around and wait to see what happened.

I wanted a future. Here in New 2. With my father. With Sebastian and my friends.

His shoulder knocked mine. "Why the frustration?"

I bumped him back. "I hate that you can read me so easily." I seemed to say that to him a lot lately, but it had become a sort of term of endearment.

He shrugged unrepentantly. "So you didn't find anything in the library this time. You've only scratched the surface of what's in there. We have three and a half years before you turn twenty-one. We'll find someone who can help us." He squeezed my hand.

I thought of the baby held by the hands of Zeus. I'd searched for it while I was in the library, but it wasn't on the table. The Keeper had seemed perplexed that it had been moved. It hadn't left the library—that much he knew. But if anyone could locate the statue, it was the Keeper.

Someone had hidden it within the library. And that someone had to be Josephine.

"I think I know why Athena killed Zeus," I said. Sebastian lifted an eyebrow, waiting for me to continue. "She had a baby that was prophesied to be the child who'd destroy Zeus. Zeus found out and took the child. I think Athena freaked and sent a god-killer, a gorgon, after him in retaliation. Only, he had the baby with him and both were turned to stone. I don't think she would've intentionally had her baby turned to stone."

"Wow," he responded with a note of disbelief. "That's . . ."

"Crazy, I know. But I'm almost sure of it. In the library there's a broken statue. The Keeper told me it's the hands of Zeus holding the baby fated to destroy him. I got a weird feeling when I saw it. Then in the main hall of the temple—"

"There's that statue of Zeus with no hands," Sebastian said, getting it. "Holy shit."

"Tell me about it. That's no ordinary statue. I'm guessing Athena was after the jar to get to the baby. Somehow she learned it was there. Maybe that's the reason the jar was given to the Novem in the first place, to hide the baby from Athena. I mean, who knows what happened after the gorgon turned them to stone, or how the statue was broken, who put it into the jar. . . ."

There were lots of unknowns, but now some of the pieces were falling into place, and there was at least a reason behind Athena's madness.

"Well," Sebastian said, "now it makes sense why she wanted you and tested you like she did. I bet she thought you could resurrect her kid."

And that made my chest hurt a little because I felt somewhat responsible for all the people my ancestors had turned to stone. The possibility that I might be able to turn them all back, to save a bunch of people, settled heavily on my conscience.

"Only problem is your grandmother," I said. "I think she knows too, or at least suspects. I looked for the statue in the library so I could touch it—"

"To turn it back?" he asked in surprise.

"No. I'd have to really pour everything I had into doing that. And I'm not even sure someone turned into stone for that long could be brought back. But if I touched it, I'd feel the gorgon's power, and then I'd know if the baby was once real."

"Which would mean the statue of Zeus is real too. Christ, imagine what would happen if you brought him back." Sebastian rubbed a hand down his face and stared out over the square. "Guess that child-fated-to-destroy-him thing came true after all."

"Yeah." Though probably not the way Zeus had thought it would. "The whole thing is kind of tragic. . . ."

"I wonder who the father was," Sebastian said.

I stared at the tiny lights bobbing on the Mississippi River, feeling that weight of responsibility again. "We should probably make sure Josephine doesn't destroy the baby or do something worse with it."

Sebastian nodded. "Her intentions can't be good."

We passed a few more seconds in thoughtful silence, the sounds from below filling the space.

"The kid *is* innocent, after all," I added.

He turned his head, a grin playing on his lips. Then he leaned over and kissed me on the mouth.

"What was that for?"

"Because you're a good person, Ari, one of the best. And because it sounds like we're about to get into trouble again."

Which translated to: Whatever happened, we were in this together. And I was pretty sure I could handle whatever life threw my way if I had my family, my friends, and Sebastian.

A smile spread over my face, and I felt it all the way to my toes. I rolled my eyes and laughed. "Said the warlock vampire to the gorgon."

Acknowledgments

Enormous gratitude to my editor, Emilia Rhodes, for her patience and insight as we went through many variations of this book. Thank you so much for always being supportive and encouraging. I have enjoyed our time together!

To all the amazing people at Simon Pulse who are or have been involved in Ari's books: Annette Pollert, Mara Anastas, Jennifer Klonsky, Carolyn Swerdloff, Dawn Ryan, Paul Crichton, Sienna Konscol, Kim Sooji, Cara Petrus, and Angela Goddard. There are many others whose names I don't yet know, but a big, big thank you to everyone. I still pinch myself at being part of the Pulse family.

To author Cynthia Cooke, for helping me immensely with this book. Here's to many more talks and lunches. Thank you for the friendship and the critique rescue.

To my agent, Miriam Kriss, who always has valuable insight and the ability to set my worries at ease. So glad to have you in my corner.

To Allen, Cheryl, Dylan, Ryan, and Isabel, and to Kami—faithful reader, sister, and friend. Thanks once again for the quick read and thoughts.

To Audrey, for dealing with all the times I stare out into space and loving me for all my quirks and stressing. You are indeed Audrey Awesomepants and seriously "Georgeous." All my love, kiddo. To Jonathan, for holding down the fort. I'm often too frazzled to express my gratitude adequately in the midst of deadlines and writing, but you bear with me all the same. Thank you!! And to James, for brightening my heart and making me laugh. You guys define my life and purpose in the best ways possible.

And finally to Melissa Marr, for her generosity and kindness, and to all the readers out there for giving Ari's books a try. Thank you for the support, the time, and the kindness. I appreciate it more than I can ever say.

About the Author

Kelly Keaton is the critically acclaimed author of *Darkness Becomes Her*. As Kelly Gay, she writes the popular adult series Charlie Madigan for Pocket Books. While she calls the Raleigh, North Carolina, area home, she can also be found chatting about books and life on Facebook and Twitter. Read more about Kelly on her website at kellykeaton.net.